Seanche's Lament

AUTHOR:
Ian McGarty

EDITOR:
Jeff Harkness

LAYOUT:
Suzy Moseby

ART DIRECTOR:
Casey Christofferson

FRONT COVER ART:
Thuan Pham

INTERIOR ART:
C.J. Marsh, Michael Syrigos, Josh Stewart, Lloyd Metcalf, Terry Pavlet, Thuan Pham, Hector Rodriguez, Brett Barkley

CARTOGRAPHY:
Robert Altbauer

PROJECT MANAGER:
Edwin Nagy

PATHFINDER CONVERSION:
Tom Knauss

©2020 Frog God Games All rights reserved. Reproduction without the written permission of the publisher is expressly forbidden. Frog God Games and the Frog God Games logo, *Seanche's Lament* is a trademark of Frog God Games, All rights reserved. All characters, names, places, items, art, and text herein are copyrighted by Frog God Games. The mention of or reference to any company or product in these pages is not a challenge to the trademark or copyright concerned.

Compatibility with the Pathfinder Roleplaying Game requires the Pathfinder Roleplaying Game from Paizo Publishing, LLC. See http://paizo.com/pathfinderRPG for more information on the Pathfinder Roleplaying Game. Paizo Publishing, LLC does not guarantee compatibility, and does not endorse this product. Pathfinder is a registered trademark of Paizo Publishing, LLC, and the Pathfinder Roleplaying Game and the Pathfinder Roleplaying Game Compatibility Logo are trademarks of Paizo Publishing, LLC, and are used under the Pathfinder Roleplaying Game Compatibility License. See http://paizo.com/pathfinderRPG/ compatibility for more information on the compatibility license This book uses the supernatural for settings, characters, and themes. All mystical and supernatural elements are fiction and intended for entertainment purposes only. Reader discretion is advised.

Frog God Games is:

Bill Webb, Matt Finch, Zach Glazar, Charles A. Wright, Edwin Nagy, Mike Badolato, and John Barnhouse

TABLE OF CONTENTS

Seanche's Lament

By Ian McGarty

A PATHFINDER ADVENTURE DESIGNED FOR FOUR TO SIX CHARACTERS OF 3RD TO 5TH LEVEL

INTRODUCTION

Seanche's Lament is an adventure for 6th to 8th level characters. The characters begin this adventure on the road, traveling in a civilized kingdom in an area with farming villages and a bucolic countryside. It is designed to be placed into any campaign you are playing but it has a decidedly Eurocentric feel due to the Irish and Celtic folklore that was explored to create it. The adventure itself is set up to follow a timeline of actions, but this is a sandbox adventure where characters may wander to whatever locations they wish. The adventure begins 18 days after a new moon as the characters arrive at the village of Fenlow.

THE STORY

The Seanche (*shana-khi*) is a legendary bard who travels the lands spreading news and joy. Stories of his musical and bardic prowess precede him. It is unclear whether Seanche is a title passed from one great performer to the next, or if the Seanche is a supernatural being who has traveled the lands for hundreds of years.

Recently, the Seanche began sharing a decidedly dark story, and the fey magic woven into these enrapturing tales is wreaking havoc in the wake of his travels. Seven years ago, the Seanche made a terrible wager, and the cursed *uilleann* (*you-lin*) *pipes of reality* (see **Appendix B**) he bears were his reward. The Seanche participated in a contest of musical skill against Gnaddr (*nadd er*), a disguised fey lord. Gnaddr knew the Seanche would win as he was the most renowned bard in a large area. Built into Gnaddr's "gift" of the *uillean pipes* was a curse that began on the new moon 18 days ago and grew in power and urgency.

Lamenting his woe, the Seanche now travels into wild and untamed lands, heading for less populated areas to minimize the damage caused by his curse and his ego. Unfortunately, the Seanche's seemingly good intentions are actually an urge created by the curse to bring the Seanche to the Eo Mughna (*eye-oh muk-na*) located deep in the Hartwood. The sadness of his curse can be seen in his eyes as he is compelled to play hauntingly beautiful songs that materialize into reality and spread the chaos that Gnaddr desires. The Seanche knows his tour of terror is coming to an end.

Gnaddr, the Serpent Priest, is a fey creature clad in scintillating green scale armor whose beauty is nearly painful to behold. He spreads an aura of charisma, and the weak-minded find it easy to simply follow his suggestions. He tricked the Seanche and forced him to use the *uillean pipes of reality* to manifest enough creatures from his nearby plane to gain a physical foothold in this realm. Even now, his power grows as the chaos increases and the veil between realms thins with the approach of the full moon. With the full moon on the eve of Imbolc (*im-olg*), the Seanche arrives at the Eo Mughna and completes the ritual. Gnaddr sacrifices the Seanche's life and musical prowess to solidify the bridge to allow Gnaddr's army to cross into this realm.

Uilleann pipes are a type of bagpipe consisting of a bellows placed under one arm, a bag, a chanter, which is often set on a piece of leather when played, three drones, and a regulator. The drones play continuously once they are switched on, while the chanter produces two octaves of notes using seven holes. Uilleann, which means elbow, refers to the bellows that is pumped to allow the bag to remain filled. A benefit of the uilleann pipes is that it allows the musician to sing while playing and it produces a rich, layered sound with a portable instrument.

GNADDR

This fey lord fancies himself The Serpent Priest. He acquired the *torc na goineog* (see **Appendix B**) from the emerald naga queen's realm and used it to force the emerald nagas to assist him. The nagas are following the exact letter of the deal they made with Gnaddr to "harass and terrify the local populace." To this end, they are simply traveling around the area in small packs and stealing tasty livestock. Strangely, the local villagers are finding valuable emeralds in the shape of scales near the sites where their livestock disappear. The populace interpreted this as a boon, although reports of giant snakes are now common.

Gnaddr's goal is to bridge the gap between this plane and his own so he can bring his army across. If his army can control this area, it weakens the veil between his plane and the Material Plane and allows his own reality to spill in and take over the area.

Gnaddr did not travel to this realm alone. Thus far, he has not managed to strengthen his hold on this realm enough to allow his army to get through. But his personal retinue and one of his lieutenants and her group of soldiers support him. He is always with his retinue of fey lupes (see **Appendix A**), although they are often hidden from view. His lieutenant, Lady Puinseann (*pun shun*, see **Appendix A**), is his hands and eyes in the land and attempts to thwart the characters if possible. If she survives earlier encounters with the characters, she is at the Hartwood with Gnaddr. If the characters delay or hamper the Seanche, Gnaddr sends a pack of 12 fey lupes to harass and hamper them. They attempt to sneak into range of the characters, attack once, and then slip away. They repeat these hit-and-run attacks until killed or driven off.

THE SEANCHE

The Seanche (see **Appendix A**) is a human man in his late 30s or early 40s. He has a well-trimmed red beard that matches his light red hair. He always carries his *uilleann pipes of reality*, which are crafted from the most exquisite honey-brown wood and fitted with gold settings, and a bag crafted from the velvet-soft hide of a white stag. His clothes are finely crafted but show the wear and stain of a life spent continuously on the road.

The Seanche's goal is to get to the Hartwood; the pipes are drawing him there and causing him to manifest a song each night. If people attempt to stop him, the pipes defend him and allow him to escape. The pipes use *stone note*, and the Seanche uses the pipe's magical spells such as *dimension door* to aid his escape.

The characters encounter the effects of the Seanche's presence for two days before they first encounter the Seanche. Barring plot-bending efforts by the characters, it takes nine more days for the Seanche to reach the Hartwood.

As the Seanche travels, he is beholden to the curse of the *uilleann pipes of reality*. The curse has several key components:

1. The Seanche may not spend more than one night in any settlement.

2. He must perform to an audience each night.

3. When traveling, he is under the effects of a *pass without trace* spell.

THE TIMELINE

The cursed Seanche overnights in Fenlow then travels for two days before the characters encounter him in Arklow. During this time, they hear rumors of his travels and see the effects of the curse. They first encounter the Seanche outside Arklow on Night 2 and see the direct manifestation of the curse the next day.

THE SEANCHE'S TRAVELS

Night	Seanche's Location	Characters' Possible Locations
1	Bandit camp outside Fenlow	Fenlow
2	A farm outside Arklow	Arklow, where they encounter the Seanche and hear *The Tale of the Magician and the Deer*
3	On the road	Chat with Fhirin and decide a course
4	Carlow	If the characters are here, they hear *The Tale of Leprechaun and the Cobbler*
5	Wicklow	If the characters are here, they hear *The Tale of Giant Pike*
6	On the road*	
7	Bru Na Brighid	If the characters are here, they hear *The Tale of the Farmer and the Leprechaun*
8	On the road*	
9	On the road*	
10	The Hartwood	Characters should catch up to the Seanche here within a few days.

* If the party is with the Seanche any of these nights, feel free to choose one of the four tales below or create your own.

If the characters catch up to him, they may travel with him for a day but each night he sings a song and triggers an encounter. These encounters always occur after the Seanche performs. Describe the tale he sings, then place the encounter in the most appropriate spot through the night and next day. Like any savvy wanderer, the Seanche attempts to trade song for a spot in a barn or around a campfire. If combat occurs, he slips away, if possible.

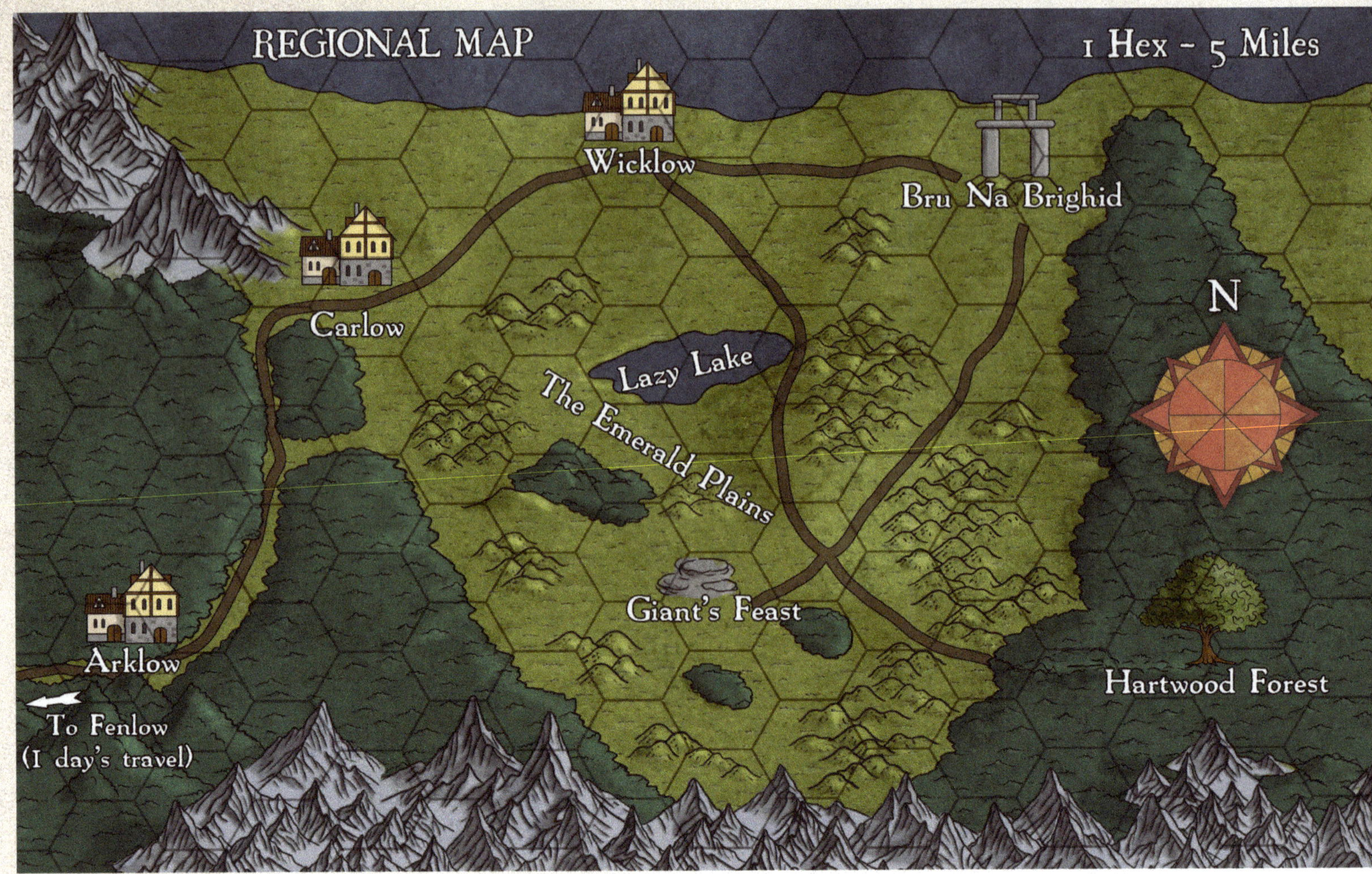

Some Stories and Associated Encounters

As the characters travel, they may find themselves in the company of the Seanche. If so, he always ends the night with a song. The following four tales can be used as the characters camp.

GAKI   **CR 7**
XP 3,200
hp 74 (*Pathfinder Roleplaying Game Bestiary 4* "Gaki")

The First Tale

The Seanche begins a woeful tale of a poor man who starved to death during a famine. He wandered the countryside, begging for the help of others. Yet, even when others offered him morsels of food and drink, the insanely jealous man loudly cursed their good fortune and bemoaned his own miserable fate, causing many of his potential benefactors to rescind their generosity. His envy ultimately sealed his fate. One day, he fell by the side of the road and died from starvation. His undiscovered and unshriven body was consumed by the land. This spirit, still hungry for food and life, now haunts unwary travelers. This creature appears to be a gaunt, emaciated figure clad in tattered clothes. Rags are wrapped around his feet, and he shuffles unsteadily with each step. He clutches a crudely carved and worn wooden bowl. If he is not offered food, he mumbles quietly to himself and shuffles off into the darkness.

Throughout the night, the group's sleep is disturbed by moaning and the shrieks of a **gaki** who walks the land on a moonless night. He casts *disguise self* to masquerade as an elderly beggar. The old man shuffles toward the characters' camp and humbly extends his bowl. If he is refused, his tattered robes begin fluttering although there is no wind. Faster and faster, they whip around him until they come to rest and reveal a gaunt, long-limbed creature with leathery skin stretched taut across an impossibly elongated jaw with a gaping toothless opening of pure blackness serving as a mouth. If destroyed, it whispers in a hoarse voice, *"Even through the ground, I hunger ..."*

The Second Tale

The Seanche sings a tale describing a handsome young man with a voice as sweet as wildflower honey. This man's arrogance and pride swell, until they and that sweet voice are all that are left of him. But these vices are his undoing, for he encounters a fey lord clad in shining green armor who claims his voice is more beautiful than the young man's. The green fey lord offers a set of uilleann pipes crafted from the most exquisite wood with gold settings and a bag crafted from the hide of a white stag.

The young man wins the contest and receives the pipes. But these beautiful pipes curse the young man to travel the land and sing the tales of curses and creatures, which allow them to materialize to terrorize people and cause chaos. He sings of a journey that ends in a dark forest at a magnificent yew with bark of silver and gold. There, the Serpent Priest forces him to sing a bridge into reality to allow a monstrous army to invade the lands. The cost of the bridge is the young man's life, and the Seanche sings of his empty husk drained of its power and life. Not even the most intrepid could stop him.

At this point, he stands and asks a question: "What will you do?" As he waits, the uilleann pipes continue their steady drone.

A successful DC 15 Perception skill check lets a character notice the similarities between the instrument the Seanche is describing and the instrument he happens to be playing. A DC 20 Knowledge (Geography) check allows the character to realize the similarities between the tree in the song and the Eo Mughna, a mighty yew in the Hartwood, a local forest.

When the Seanche asks the characters what they will do, he activated the song and left a magical duplicate of himself to deal with the characters. If they are aggressive, have them roll initiative and begin the battle with a **Shadow Seanche** (see **Appendix A**).

THE THIRD TALE

The Seanche sings a tale of three fey sisters who lived in the forest near a village. They had lived in those woods for longer than men had been near. But as the village grew, the forest was cleared by the villagers and consumed by a growing urban settlement. The fey sisters were corrupted and turned into twisted perversions of what they once were.

The next day, 3 **bog nixies** ambush the characters.

BOG NIXIE (3)　　　　**CR 3**
XP 800
hp 19; (*Pathfinder Roleplaying Game Bestiary 3* "Nixie, Bog")

THE FOURTH TALE

On this dark and cool night with a view of the nearly full moon, the Seanche joins you at the fire once again. With an apologetic look and a sigh, he brings out the beautiful uilleann pipes and begins a song. This strange song has a discordant melody that echoes into the night as the Seanche begins a song of the Moon being lonely each night and longing for someone to spend time within the darkness. She enacts a plan that severs the shadows from Brighid's followers. The shadows dance with her each night but when Brighid finds out, she flies to the Moon's palace on a horse of fire and demands the shadows back. The Moon acquiesces and returns the shadows, but her immense sadness touches Brighid's heart. She tells the Moon that she will force the Sun to stay alight while the Moon visits as often as possible. This is why we sometimes see the Moon in the mornings or afternoons.

"Behind you," the Seanche whispers as tears fall from his eyes.

The shadows of the characters are severed from their bodies and immediately attack. A **severed shadow** (see **Appendix A**) copy of each character exists. Apply the "Shadow Creature" template from the **Pathfinder Roleplaying Game Bestiary 4** to each of the characters to create these severed shadows. When the battle begins, the Seanche slips off into the night, if possible.

THE ADVENTURE BEGINS

The adventure begins on the road as the characters travel toward another destination. The roads in this area are wide dirt paths with occasional stretches of cobblestone or gravel in the wettest areas. It is clear someone regularly maintains the road. The locals are preparing to celebrate Imbolc, a festival to welcome spring. This festival also honors the local deity Brighid, who is a goddess of poets, smiths, and healers. She often appears clad is bronze armor and wreathed in flames or sunlight. The local people are excited this year due to the early thaw; crops are already sprouting in the fields.

1. FENLOW

The first signs of an approaching village materialize on the horizon. Farmers and workers are in the fields, and animals graze in pens or are tended by shepherds. The people are friendly, and children and adults alike offer a friendly wave. The village proper is small and quaint. A general store, a tavern with generous outdoor seating, a stable and blacksmith, and a 30-foot-tall stone tower sit alongside the well-worn dirt road. Chickens, dogs, and cats wander the town looking for refuse.

Standing outside the tower are a young man in chainmail holding a spear and an older, thickly bearded man with clothes made of fine materials worn with age and use, vestiges of a wealth that seems to have faded. The young man is talking animatedly, gesturing with his free hand and pointing toward the forest.

A Perception skill check can be made to overhear some of the guards' conversation. With a DC 10 check, the party learns that a boy is missing. If the characters pursue the matter further, they learn the following details with successful Knowledge (local) checks. On a DC 12 check, they learn that he's been kidnapped, but he's also at home. On a DC 15 check, they learn that a fey creature replaced the local boy with a changeling. If somebody makes a successful DC 18 check, the party learns that the young guard discovered an area in the forest where the fey are entering and saw the missing boy and a fey lord with his retinue.

Speaking with anyone in the village reveals the following to the characters:

1. A famous bard known as the Seanche passed through the village yesterday afternoon. He shared news of the kingdom, local area gossip, and sang songs and shared a story.
2. Last night, the Seanche shared a story about a farmer's son who was kidnapped by the fey and replaced with a changeling. The local kids are playing out the story in the streets.
3. A village less than a week away captured a leprechaun and acquired his gold. But now mysterious tragedies are occurring in the town.
4. The Seanche shared a story of a cursed poet who angered a dryad and was forced to watch as the tales he sang became real. In the story, the poet dies alone, hiding in a cave for fear of harming someone.
5. The predicted light snows and mild winter led to early crops and excitement in the area. It is a good year for the villages in the area.
6. Giant snake swarms have been seen in the area but they haven't harmed anyone yet.
7. Tommy Riordan found three huge flat emeralds in his cattle pen after three goats went missing. He thinks brownies left him a gift after taking the animals.

1-B. A COURT OF THE FEY

The young guardsman immediately offers to accompany the characters to the area in the forest where he saw the fey lord holding court. It was in the deep forest, and the guardsman explains that even the most experienced woodsfolk lose their way reaching the area and getting back. To follow the trail with only verbal guidance from the young man requires a successful DC 20 Survival skill check. It takes three hours to reach the fey lord's impromptu court.

The forest is a tangle of undergrowth and tree limbs as you struggle to keep pace with the young guard. He pauses every few moments to allow the slower members of the group the opportunity to catch up but he coaxes them along each time. Without warning, the thick forest breaks open into a clearing roughly 50 feet across. A small stream gurgles its way across an edge of this clearing, and a handsome elf with aquiline features holds his nose haughtily in the air as he watches your group stumble into the clearing. Several figures in intricate armor crafted of some sort of metallic leaves stand around the edges of the clearing, and a woven basket sits beside the fey lord's ornate and beautifully carved wooden throne. A small baby coos and gurgles happily in its wicker bassinet as it nestles amid lush green leaves sprouting from still-living branches.

The **fey lord** (see **Appendix A**) kidnapped this child but may be convinced to release the boy. He does so in exchange for any of the following: a replacement child, a magical item, or one year of a character's life.

> "Aaah, visitors! Welcome to my impromptu spring court. I assume you have come to show obeisance at my feet? The village has already gifted me this beautiful child. It will be a strong addition to the servants of my court. Perhaps you are also here to pledge your fealty and join my retinue?" The fey lord speaks in a haughty and demeaning manner.

The fey lord is manipulative in his negotiations and attempts to use language to sweeten the deal in his favor. The characters may also attempt to put a loophole into whatever options they present and should be rewarded for creativity and cleverness (e.g., the chaste cleric offers her firstborn child).

If the encounter turns to combat, the fey lord is in his lair and protected by a retinue of well-armed and highly trained warriors (8 **steel elves**, see **Appendix A**).

If the characters are able to return the child, the town rewards them 50 gp and the lord gifts them a family heirloom. This may be any *+1 weapon* you determine.

2. TRAVELING TO THE NEXT VILLAGE

Travel in this idyllic countryside is occasionally interrupted by wild or dangerous animals and even the occasional group of bandits. Read the following to the party as the day turns to night and they seek out a camp:

> Ahead, a dented and scratched cart has been pulled to the side of the road and a small fire blazes nearby. Half a dozen humanoids in worn clothes and armed with a hodgepodge of secondhand weapons and scraps of armor mill around the flames. They appear to be arguing.

The bandits spot any characters who approach and don't succeed at a DC 13 Stealth skill check. Details of the argument can be heard with a DC 13 Perception skill check. The information that can be gleaned is as follows:

- The bean fionn (*be-on-fin*), the White Lady, took Albrecht below the nearby lake to drown tonight when the moon shines brightest.
- The men are arguing about whether to rescue Albrecht or if they could give the bean fionn something else to appease her.
- The bandits spent yesterday evening with a traveling bard who sang to them of the failure of the Lazy One, a fey creature who was off with her human lover rather than guarding a local spring. This caused extensive flooding across the countryside. The fey creature blamed the people of the land for causing this and is said to have drowned her love in order to take him into the Tuatha De Danann (*to-ah day dun-on*) to live with her forever.
- Albrecht is the only one who knows where the bandit treasure is hidden. The remaining bandits are about to draw lots to determine who's going to replace Albrecht and who's going to parley with the bean fionn.

The bean fionn is a beautiful humanoid who lives in the water of the nearby pond. A small island camouflaged in trees and plant growth sits in the center of this pond, and an aged wooden skiff is pulled onto the rocky beach and tied to a large boulder nearby. A character who succeeds at a DC 14 Perception or Knowledge (Nature) skill check notices that the water appears to be rising. The boat is floating, no longer perched on the shore where it was left. At first it almost appears as though there is a tide, but no obvious inlets exist to create a current. If the pond is observed for a short time, it becomes quite clear that the water is rising, and quickly.

Anyone disturbing the water or wildlife near the pond summons the **bean fionn** (see **Appendix A**), who arrives with a bubbling of water. She does not notice characters who make a successful DC 15 Stealth skill check.

The bean fionn forms from the water itself, a whirling tower of water that coalesces into a beautiful humanoid woman with pronounced elven features and exceptionally long ears. Her skin remains so pale that it is nearly blue. She speaks in a melodious voice that sparkles like soft chimes with any who approach, offering them fabulous wealth in exchange for a year in her service. In order to free the mortal she captured, she needs to be bested in some contest.

The bean fionn is smart, coldhearted, and prone to tricking characters. She offers the characters a straight exchange of one mortal soul for another but accepts a reasonable challenge provided by the characters. This takes some ingenuity and creativity on your part. If a skill challenge is offered, the bean fionn cheats and augment her abilities by granting herself a 1d6 bonus to any skill check. If she feels cheated or dislikes the results, she may simply attack. If she is attacked, she immediately emits a high-pitched

whistle that summons her pack of 4 **phookas**. They understand that this means she is under attack and attempt to surprise her opponents by *tree striding* into positions to surprise and ambush the characters. If the bean fionn is defeated, her lair may be discovered by diving below the water and succeeding on a DC 16 Perception skill check. Her lair is beyond a cave entrance that opens into a small grotto lush with plants, small cascading pools, and beds of strand strewn with random personal items. Items are tucked into the stone walls or sit on shelves where there are no plants. Most of these items are mundane items from the mortal realm that she has collected. But tucked among this hodgepodge of items are a *helm of underwater action* and a *bag of holding, type II* containing seven assorted gems worth 35 gp each. The bean fionn's captured human is also lying on a sandbar, glassy eyed and confused. This charm wears off once he is free of the bean fionn's lair.

PHOOKA (3)   **CR 3**
XP 800
hp 22 (*Tome of Horrors Complete* "Phooka")

INTERACTING WITH THE FEY

The fey are selfish and capricious, always seeking favor and advantage. Due to their long lives, they are willing to play a long game in order to get what they want. Ideally, they draw anyone they deal with into their stories and goals, making them characters in the play and story tropes that they must re-enact. They may be found acting out older legends and stories with new victims. Their glamour and charisma are palpable and infectious, which is why many common folk find themselves pulled into a fey creature's plans before they realize they had a chance to escape. They are fickle and can be emotionally unpredictable, shifting from carefree and laughing to anger and violence in the blink of an eye. But they also crave interaction and the adoration of humans and demihumans, and they seem to somehow gain strength from these interactions. The following guidelines are recommended when roleplaying any interaction with the fey:

- They gain a +5 circumstance bonus on Bluff, Diplomacy, and Sense Motive skill checks.
- Characters suffer a −5 circumstance penalty on Bluff, Diplomacy, and Sense Motive skill checks made against them.
- If the characters "win" an encounter with a fey creature, it may be because they are fulfilling a trope or a need for the story that the fey is attempting to recreate.

3. ARKLOW

> This small cluster of stone and wooden buildings is nestled amid rolling hills and verdant farmland. Children run between buildings and play in the open spaces. Arklow consists of a roadside public house, a grain mill alongside a river that cuts through town, a general store, and several homes. Worked fields and farmhouses surround the village itself. Animals idly meander through the green fields.
>
> A great deal of noise comes from the public house, where you hear the joyful buzz of people gathering, laughing, talking, and playing music.

The public house is packed with people, and any movement through this dense crowd of people is the same as moving through difficult terrain.

The characters enter just as a man in a rich brown doublet that has seen years of wear despite being well cared for takes the stage (**Seanche**, see **Appendix A**). His face appears jovial, with a wide smile, but his eyes are deep emerald pools that are worn with sorrow. He has a well-trimmed red beard that matches his light red hair. He holds his uilleann pipes in his lap. He begins tuning the instrument, pumping the bag with his arm and elbow, and the crowd hushes themselves. Allow the characters time to get a drink and table and to carouse awhile.

The man begins singing a sweet and mournful ballad that immediately silences the crowd. His voice and the instrument combine to create a harmonious coupling that nears perfection.

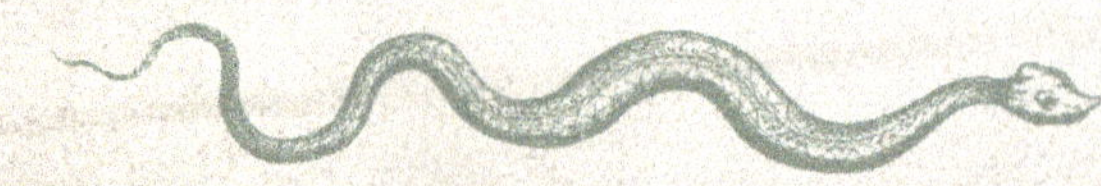

A character may attempt a Spellcraft skill check to discover what is happening. Consult the table below:

DC	Effect Noticed
10	There is something magical about this tune.
14	The effect is not influencing people but it is drawing something from them.
16	The effect of the magic emanating from the lute and this man's voice is drawing some power or lifeforce in small portions from everyone in the crowd.

The music doesn't cause any lasting damage but anyone who fails a DC 15 Fortitude saving throw becomes exhausted.

The song describes a young person who lost his wife when an evil magician turned her into a deer for seven years. When he finally caught the magician, he found that the mage had killed and eaten his wife, but the child she was carrying escaped as a deer.

The Seanche moves to a table and begins sharing news of neighboring villages and the kingdom. The characters may speak to him, and this is an excellent spot to insert future adventure hooks, news of your campaign world, and general rumors. You can also use the generic rumor table below:

1d8	Rumor
1	A terrifying leviathan has been harassing fishing vessels along the coast and destroying nets and traps.
2	A farmer in a nearby village is said to have created a truly delightful whiskey this year.
3	The tax collector was spotted a few weeks away, right on schedule.
4	It is nearly mating season for the local deer, and it looks to be a healthy herd this year.
5	Fungus infected the crops of several nearby farmers, and they may be looking for spare seed on loan or for coin if they must.
6	Sam Hasting had a cow go missing last week but he found a huge strangely cut and valuable emerald in the pen. A fey must have taken the cow and left him the gift.
7	The child of a wealthy nearby landowner is coming of age in several months and they are hearing out potential suitors.
8	Wolves have been chasing people in the Hartwood.

The crowd clears well before midnight, and the people leave tired but happy. The bard disappears with the crowd to a room provided by the house. He leaves in the morning before the characters notice. They may spot him if extreme measures and some creativity are supplied by the characters and paired with a successful DC 25 Perception skill check. If so, he can be seen disappearing into the darkness under the shroud of his *pass without trace* spell. The faint melody of a vaguely familiar tune can be heard carried on the breeze as he departs.

If the characters continue their journey on the road, they happen across a large farm with outbuildings and smaller houses placed among the fields. The main farmstead contains several buildings within a five-foot-high stone wall made from gathered fieldstones. A commotion is occurring in front of the buildings with men and women shouting and arming themselves with convenient field tools and a few older swords or spears. As the characters approach, people can be overheard talking about hunting and killing the doirche (*door-ka*) who cast the curse.

"We know where he is, I say we burn him out!"

"Yeah! … We can't let this stand."

"He could come back and turn any of us!"

"Let's go!"

This mob of angry villagers is armed with a variety of farming implements, several rusty swords, and axes. A successful DC 12 Sense Motive skill check identifies the fear and concern in this group. They appear to be genuine in those feelings and without apparent duplicitousness. Speaking with the group reveals that a magician turned the young farmer's wife into a deer yesterday evening. They tracked the magician to a cave in the nearby bog only an hour or two away.

If the characters rescue the wife before the magician kills her, they can lift the curse. If they do so, the farmers reward them with an heirloom from the family (a *ring of protection*) as well as 500 gp worth of assorted coins. The group sends **Rory Shalgur** (see "Novice Scout" in the *Pathfinder Roleplaying Game NPC Codex*), an adept hunter and tracker who is familiar with the area, to guide the characters. They explain that this stretch of woods can be difficult to navigate, especially lately with things seeming to shift occasionally. If the characters wish to go alone, Rory provides directions and the players can make a DC 20 Survival skill check. If they are successful, they locate the doirche's cave. If they fail, they end up back at the edge of the forest where the villagers are waiting.

DOIRCHE'S CAVE

As the characters approach the cave, they spot bone totems placed around the area and hung with chimes made from larger leg and arm bones. A successful DC 18 Heal or Knowledge (Nature) skill check identifies the bones as those of various animals, goblins, and orcs. The guide remains just beyond the first totem as he points out the cave ahead, which seems to sprout from the bog and provides an island that drops into the peat around it.

1. CAVE ENTRANCE

This small rock- and peat-walled cave seems to absorb noise. An iron brazier hanging from the ceiling sputters and hisses as it casts dim light through this room. Crude glyphs and pictographs are carved into the walls, and two exits veer off in nearly opposite directions.

2. SKINNING ROOM

The coppery scent of aged blood tweaks your nose and tingles on your tongue as you enter this room. A crude wooden table with a variety of skinning and butcher knives rest in a pottery bowl. The tabletop is dark with bloodstains and marred with numerous cuts and gouges. Several hides are stretched across the walls and held in place with wooden pegs. There are no other exits from this room.

3. PEAT MAZE

This maze-like series of tunnels is studded with long dead, desiccated bodies buried in the peat. Their leathery skin and clothes are preserved but bear a ruddy hue that matches the red hair upon their heads. With a successful DC 15 Knowledge (Nature) skill check, a character notes the red coloration is due to an extended stay in a grave of peat. A total of 13 desiccated and withered bodies, both men and women, are in the room. You can determine their races to best match your campaign and setting. These bodies are all cursed by the doirche, and each has a silver amulet beneath their clothes that is slightly sunken into their skin. This pendant is etched with intricate runes that a successful Knowledge (Arcana) DC 16 determines to be the source of their curse. While the characters examine the bodies, 4 **shadows** attack. Casting *dispel magic* (DC 20 dispel check), *dispel evil*, or *remove curse* on a body and amulet destroys a corresponding shadow and releases the body's trapped soul. Casting any spell that creates light directly at the bodies stuns the shadow for the duration of the spell. If the shadows are destroyed, they rematerialize in 1d4 x 10 minutes unless the bodies are destroyed, too. If the bodies are destroyed, the amulets lose their magical aura but may be recovered and are worth 19 gp each.

SHADOW (4)　　　**CR 3**
XP 800
hp 19 (*Pathfinder Roleplaying Game Bestiary* "Shadow")

4. STORAGE ROOM

This large cave is brimming with small shelves, gourds, and jars hanging from twine in the ceiling. The ceiling is only eight feet high at its tallest and irregularly shaped. This limits the use of large two-handed weapons, and you may impose disadvantage at your discretion. A large iron cauldron rests on stones, and hot coals smolder beneath it. The air is hazy with smoke and reduces visibility. The smoke is thick and pungent with the smell of burnt peat. The 2 **doirches** (see **Appendix A**) stands ready to engage the party and holds an action to cast a spell when he first sees the group. If the group simply destroys the doirches, it will be difficult for them to find the proper incantation to return the cursed farmer's wife to her true form. A successful DC 20 Perception skill check finds the incantation scrawled on a veiny vellum sheet in a spidery script. If a doirche is subdued, he exchanges his life for the information the party seeks. Alternatively, if the party attempts to use diplomacy and parleys with the doirches from the start, they lift the curse if the characters bring them the cursed woman who is currently in the form of a deer. However, a doirche requires a gift worth 50 gp in exchange for his services.

Tracking the deer is a difficult task, but the guide who remained waiting can help. He knows the land and gains a +2 competence bonus on Knowledge (Geography) and Survival skill checks made within these woods. He can also give the Aid Another action to a character tracking the deer. As the characters follow the deer, the tracks of large wolves begin appearing in the area. Rustling in the trees can be heard as the wolfpack begins its hunt. The characters must complete three successful challenges in six attempts or their encounter with the **wolfpack** (see below) starts with the party at a disadvantage. Using spells and creativity in the face of these challenges should be rewarded with circumstance and luck bonuses. Some directionality is suggested in the writing of these challenges, but that is only to create a sense of chase with the characters; it does not matter which way the characters go as they continue to experience challenges. Each time the characters encounter a challenge, they also need to continue to successfully track the deer with a DC 18 Survival check. If they fail to track the deer, they suffer a –2 circumstance penalty to overcome their next obstacle because they were moving too quickly and without caution.

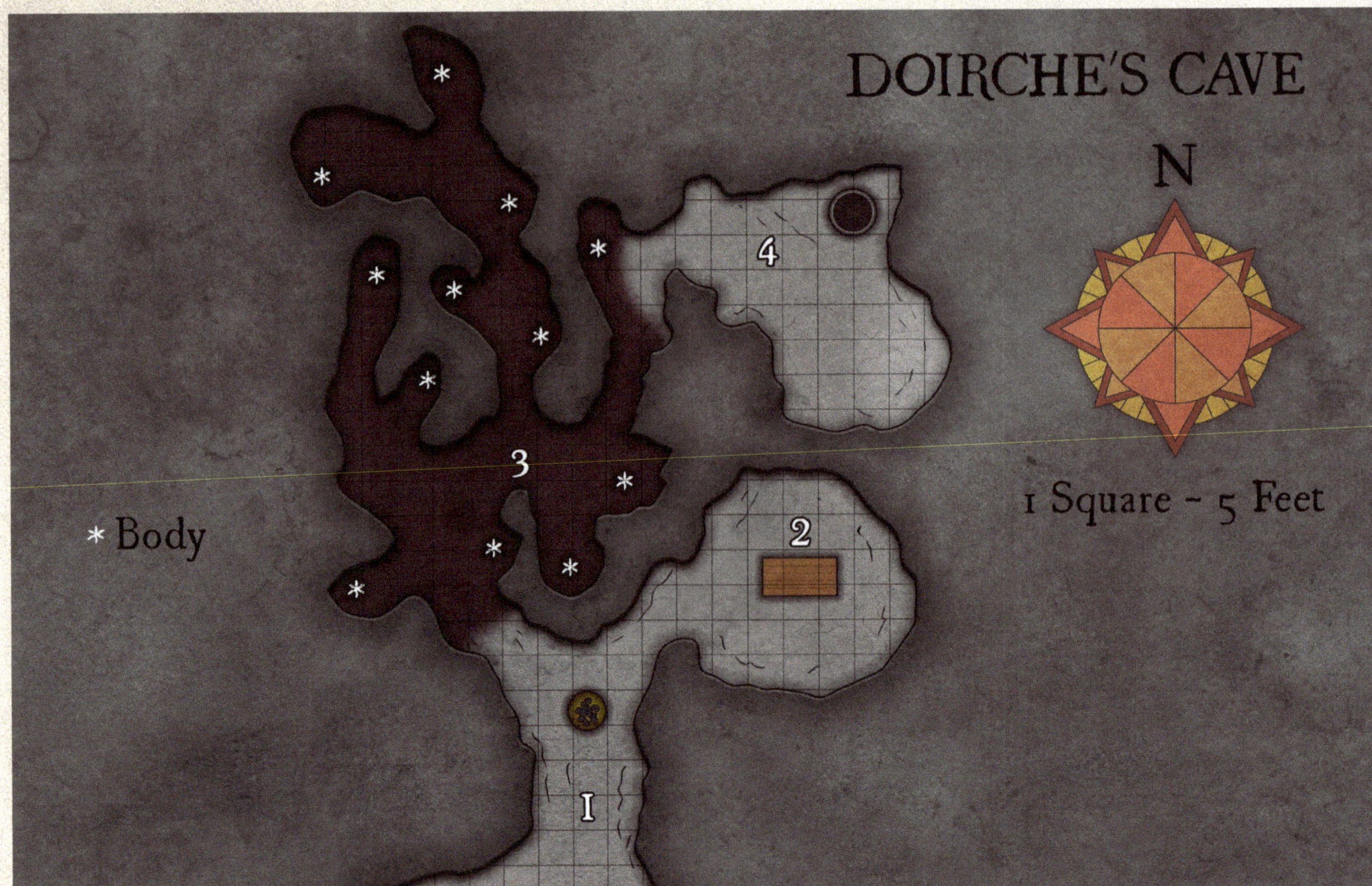

CHALLENGES WHILE TRACKING

1. THE STREAM

The tracks of the deer lead to a shallow, 20-foot-wide stream interspersed with rocks and fallen trees. The tracks of the deer run parallel to the water before disappearing. The deer entered the water and then doubled back, where it crossed to the other side.

Finding the trail requires a successful DC 18 Perception or Survival skill check, though it takes a successful Survival skill check to follow the tracks. If the trail cannot be found, the characters press on in the direction they believe the deer went. If they are reticent to pick a direction, allow a character to notice movement in a particular direction to encourage them to keep moving.

2. THE BUZZING STUMP

Anyone nearing the edge of this small clearing can attempt a DC 15 Perception skill check to discern a faint buzzing.

The buzzing emanates from a 12-foot-tall rotted tree stump that succumbed to a lightning strike some time ago. It now serves as a hive for swarms of wasps.

Each round on Initiative 20, the wasps make a Wisdom (Perception) check to determine if they see the characters. If they do, 1d4 **wasp swarms** exit the hive and make a beeline toward the character(s) who were noticed. An additional 1d4 wasp swarms spawn each time a character is noticed. Each character may cause only 1d4 wasp swarms to spawn.

WASP SWARM   CR 3
XP 800
hp 31 (*Pathfinder Roleplaying Game Bestiary* "Wasp Swarm")

3. SALTY BROWNIES

Several foot-tall humanoids with lithe and wiry bodies and clothing of drab browns and greens are sitting at a small table laden with dozens of tiny platters. With tiny cries and shouts of anger, they defend their party.

Unless one of the characters makes a successful DC 16 Perception skill check, they stomp into a party of doll-sized creatures and incur the wrath and ire of 8 **brownies**. The brownies not pursue the characters if they attempt to escape. If the brownies engage in combat, an additional 1d8 brownies arrive each round and join the fracas.

BROWNIE (8)   CR 1
XP 200
hp 4 (*Pathfinder Roleplaying Game Bestiary 2* "Brownie")

4. Thick Hedges

> The deer's trail leads directly into a thicket of vicious-looking thorns that appears nearly impassable.

A successful DC 18 Acrobatics check is needed to slip through the thorns unscathed. Failure deals 2d4 points of damage. Any creative ideas to avoid or deal with the thorns should be rewarded. Magic may also be an acceptable solution, and solutions using reasonable spells and 1st-level or higher slots should be allowed to solve this problem.

5. Mud Pit

> The flat area ahead is covered in a blanket of wet leaves that obscures the deep soft mud beneath. The tracks of the deer cross the clearing and exit onto a game trail on the other side.

A DC 20 Survival skill check spots this area of soft mud obscured by leaves. If the characters cross, they immediately sink waist deep into soft mud and ends up pinned. A character can use a standard action to make a DC 20 Escape Artist skill check or Strength check to either escape or pull another creature out. A creature stuck in the mud takes 1d6 points of damage at the end of each round.

6. The Drop

> The deer's trail immediately plummets down a steep, forested incline. The dead leaves covering this sharp decline make footing treacherous.

Each character must immediately make a successful DC 15 Reflex saving throw or suffer 2d6 points of damage as they crash into trees, through saplings, and off rocks in their plummet down the hill. Each character must succeed on two consecutive DC 15 Acrobatics or Climb skill checks to reach the bottom safely. Each failure causes 2d6 points of damage. They may attempt to use spells to assist them but need to make a successful Concentration check to cast while tumbling down the hill.

The Wolfpack

The characters encounter 10 **fey lupes** (see **Appendix A**). If the characters did not succeed with at least three of the six challenges as they tracked the deer, this combat is already underway, and the **deer** has just 1 hit point remaining and is surrounded by wolves. Otherwise, the characters arrive just as the wolves begin circling the deer. A successful DC 14 Survival or Knowledge (Nature) skill check identifies these creatures as atypical and not wolves that traditionally roam the area. These wolves are larger, with dark fur that bristles along their spines. Their slavering jaws are filled with rows of sharp teeth that drip in anticipation of a meal. Their yellow eyes seem to contain a spark of intelligence. Tactically, they focus on knocking a single creature to the ground and press their advantage with as many pack members as possible. The wolves attack the deer if no other targets are near, but they turn on the party as soon as they arrive. If the deer survives, it placidly follows the characters back to the doirches to be cured or it allows a spellcaster to complete the ritual to restore it. Upon dispelling the curse, the doirches vanishes in a shower of golden sparks, leaving the wife of the farmer in her original form.

HERD ANIMAL, DEER   CR 1/4
XP 100
hp 11 (*Tome of Horrors Complete*, "Deer")

4. A Forked Tongue in the Path

> After leaving the second village and dealing with the doirches, you find yourselves leaving the hilly grassland as the dirt road leads into a thick, shadowy forest populated with ancient gnarled and twisted trees. After entering the first shadows of cool shade, a small clearing appears, and the path forks off in two directions. A large willow tree shades the clearing as its long limbs drape a curtain of greenery across the area.

An emerald naga is concealed in the willow and can be spotted with a successful DC 24 Perception skill check.

As the characters enter the clearing, the sibilant voice of Fhirin (*fi reen*) the **emerald naga** (see **Appendix A**) cautions them, "A sssssplit in your pathhhhh, perhapsssss." Fhirin then lowers herself from the tree and coils herself at the edge of the clearing.

"That way issssss danger, cursesssssss, and dark fey magic," Fhirin gestures to the path on the left with her tail. "Or you can choosssssse lifffffffe and ffffffffreedom." She gestures to the path on her right. "I leave it up to you." Fhirin is prepared for aggressive characters. Her goal, if the characters fight, is to poison as many characters as possible and then escape into the thick forest. Her instructions and the *geas/quest* that compel her are to slow anyone who follows the same path as the Seanche. Fhirin only follows the letter of the *geas/quest* she is under, as she does not like being compelled to do anything. Gnaddr has been dominating serpentkind across the countryside for several months, building toward something Fhirin does not want to hang around for.

Fhirin speaks with the characters and answers questions, although she is evasive. She may reveal the following:

- Gnaddr knows the language of serpents and the whispers of their secrets. He wears the *torc na goineog* (*tork na go-nee-yolk*), which grants him primacy over all serpentkind and is the item that binds the emerald naga queen here.
- The emerald naga queen is angry that Gnaddr is driving them to war with the people of the region. She has the ear of Brighid, who may grant a boon to those she favors.
- Imbolc is fast approaching and will be a time of weal and woe.
- She repeats this Imbolc prayer:

> *The serpent will come from the hole*
> *On the brown Day of Bríde,*
> *Though there should be three feet of snow*
> *On the flat surface of the ground*
>
> —*Gaelic Proverb*

- The Emerald Naga Queen SS'Thissk can be found at the Giant's Table. She loves ebony jewelry and gems.

If the characters continue on the left path following the Seanche, the road takes them to Carlow.

If the characters choose the path to the right, they soon emerge from the forest into the Emerald Plains with Tabla An-Mohr being the most obvious place in front of them.

5. Carlow

> As the trees thin ahead, a small village nestled in lush green hills and surrounded by neatly tended crops is visible several miles ahead. Advancing, the path slowly turns into a well-maintained cobblestone road with hedgerows rise alongside it. Carlow's center is set around a crossroads lined with a dozen thatch-roofed houses and business, notably an inn and tavern, a cobbler, a blacksmith, a baker, and a general goods store. A fountain gurgles in the small square in the center of town, and well-tended flower bushes can be seen around the village. A rhythmic *tap-tap-tapping* and *clang* of metal provides a steady rhythm as you approach the tavern. Several large tables are set out front.

These table are empty before lunch, have 1d4 patrons in the afternoons, and 2d6 patrons in the evenings.

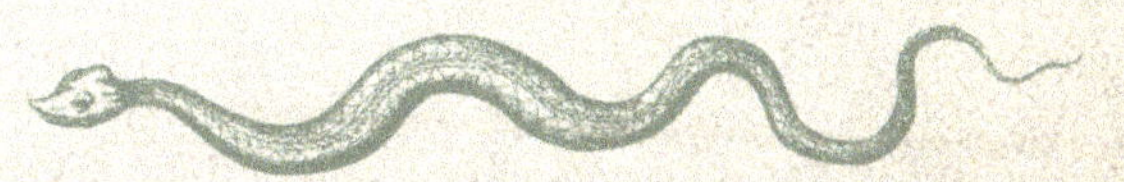

A wooden sign showing signs of recent touchups hangs above the door of this thatch-roofed stone building with a wattle-and-daub second story showing exposed beams. A wooden flowerbox sprouts red and gold tulips below a wide bay window with several well-crafted pairs of shoes, including a pair of supple high-calf brown leather boots with a gleaming brass buckle, a pair of ankle-height red leather shoes with golden buttons and clasps, and a pair of sturdy black leather shoes meant for a child. The interior of the shop is cluttered and dark but cozy. A large workbench contains scraps of leather, wooden soles of various sizes, nails and brads, and a pair of well-cared-for tools. A short man with wild brown hair, a pair of brass spectacles, and a brown leather apron carefully taps, nailing leather to the sole of a shoe.

Leath Brogan (NG, male human, Wis 15; Exp 6; Profession [cobbler] +11) is a soft-spoken man who always has a slightly manic smile on his face. He calls out to anyone who enters and takes a moment to get his work to a point where he may successfully pause. He is highly regarded as the finest cobbler in the area. One can spend nearly as much as desired on a pair of shoes here, but a sturdy pair of reliable shoes can be had for 2 sp. Custom work with fine leathers and expensive adornments can run as much as 250 gp. Leath always has about a dozen pairs of shoes prepared in a variety of common sizes. They range in price from 2 sp to 28 gp. Leath is transformed into the mythical Leprechaun spoken of later that night in the Seanche's cursed song.

Roughly hewn wooden tables and benches sit in front of this two-story stone building with a thatch roof. Your eyes are immediately drawn to the bronze face hung above the door. The interior of the Wizard's Weal is dark with a low ceiling made more precarious with the visible wooden beams. A six-foot span of dark polished wood shows the signs and stains of years of steady use. Several shelves on the wall behind the bar contain bottles of spirits, wine, and liqueurs. Three kegs rest in cradles below the shelves. Small glowing stones are hung about the room and create a soft glow of amber and yellow lights. The man behind the bar is an exceedingly tall elf wearing a purple and black robe with crudely stitched silver stars. His face lights up when he sees you. "I am Findolin! The proprietor of the Wizard's Weal. Might I interest you in one of our arcane alchemical libations? Or have you come to gaze upon the mysterious brazen head?" Findolin gestures to a bronze face set into the stone above the fireplace.

With a successful DC 16 Knowledge (Arcana or Religion) skill check, the runes are found to be only facsimiles of "best guesses" of runes or even completely made up symbols that have an arcane feel; in other words, they are fakes. Findolin regularly makes flawed attempts to sound wise and wizardly, and is quick to offer his newest "elixir" or concoction created from mixing his large collection of spirits and liqueurs with seeming randomness. He often attempts to entice customers with the newest item he has muddled for a drink, and the items are often surprising or food adjacent, like soil that grew a rare variety of mushroom.

The Brazen Head

The bronze face, or brazen head, is approximately three feet wide and four feet long. The face is a man with an aquiline nose, thick curly beard, and high cheekbones. He wears a cowl with intricate patterns decorating the edges. If a *detect magic* is used, the face radiates a steady aura of divination, transmutation, evocation, and enchantment magics. The face may be activated by using a standard action to speak command words while placing an offering in its mouth.

There are two commands for the face. Both of the command words needed to activate the brazen head are etched into the bar glasses. A beer can be obtained for 5 cp and once it is finished, the command words "slainte chugaibh" (*slawn-cha hoo-uv*, "health to you [all]") are seen carefully etched into the glass. A glass of whiskey can be ordered for 1 gp, and the bottom of this glass proclaims, "slainte agus tainte" (*slawn-cha ogg-uss tawn-cheh*, "health and wealth").

The face accepts offerings to empower itself. If someone is boosted to its mouth, it opens and a flat bronze tongue grinds out, waiting. Placing gemstones, coins, or enchanted items on the tongue and speaking the command words activate the face.

It has the ability to:

* Answer a question regarding any event that occurs in the next seven days within 50 miles using a short phrase or sentence. This costs 25 gp worth of valuable items that can be fit into the brazen head's mouth. There is no limit to the number of times this may be used, and it is always successful.

* Answer any yes or no question. This power has a cumulative 10% failure rate each time it is used. For example, the first try has a 0% chance of failure, the second has a 10% chance, the third a 20% chance, and so on. A failure results in no answer. This costs 75 gp worth of valuables that can be fit into the brazen head's mouth.

The brazen head has always been an object of wonder in this village, and some believe the tavern and village grew up around it. The locals believe that it protects and blesses them. They tell a story about how it commanded a swindling peddler to leave the village in a booming voice with cracks of thunder, darkening clouds, and flashes of lightning. In truth, this item was created more than 900 years ago by the wizard Mor Kegan to demonstrate to her on again, off again partner what a useful man looked like. Since then, it has been involved in predicting several curses, forewarning precipitous calamities, and revealing the location of a grand treasure.

The Seanche in Carlow

The Seanche enters Carlow on the fourth day of the adventure. If the characters are present that evening, they enjoy the following encounter:

When the Seanche enters Carlow, he heads to the Wizard's Weal and trades his musical talents for a drink, a meal, and a spot in the stables overnight. He tunes and begins his set with several rowdy ballads and requests from the audience, which quickly grows in size once the townsfolk realize a bard is performing.

His performance is exceptional and ends with a rollicking tale of a little man in a red vest and red tricorn hat. The man was the finest cobbler in the area. An ugly, squat, fey creature with a round face known as Luricawne wagered the little man that he was a better cobbler. Both of these skilled craftsmen worked all night, tapping away at soles, stretching leather, attaching buttons and clasps. But when it was over, the little man in the red vest was clearly the winner. Luricawne was angry but handed the little man the gold he had wagered and then said, "Your shoes are so fine, they make their own music." After this, the cobbler began boasting to everyone about his skill and about how he was a better cobbler than even mystical creatures. This angered Luricawne when he heard it, so he hatched a plan. He toiled for nine days and nine nights and built perhaps the finest shoe hammer ever crafted. It was silver and etched with scrolling leaf work. Despite its tremendous delicacy, it struck with the force of a much larger hammer, driving a nail into the sole of a shoe in a single tap.

Luricawne left the hammer on the door of the cobbler with a note that read, "The finest tool for the finest cobbler. May all your shoes be good enough to dance in!" The cobbler was overjoyed and immediately began making shoes with the hammer. After nearly a month of building the finest shoes for his neighbors, the full moon rose, and with it, the shoes awoke. They sought out the feet of their masters and took them dancing into the moonlight. Most people awoke the next day confused, in strange places, and with extremely sore feet. From that day forward, the cobbler was ruined, and nobody wanted his fabulous dancing shoes.

A character may make a Knowledge (Arcana) check to discover what is happening during the performance. Consult the table below.

DC	Effect Noticed
10	There is something magical about this tune.
14	The effect is not influencing the people but it is drawing something from them.
18	The effect of the magic emanating from the lute and this man's voice is drawing some power or life force in small portions from everyone in the crowd.

The music doesn't cause any lasting damage but anyone who fails a DC 15 Fortitude saving throw becomes exhausted.

The next morning, anyone in the village who is wearing shoes made by Leath Brogan must make a DC 18 Will saving throw or be forced to dance. The villagers begin dancing their way to the town's center where Leath Brogan has transformed into a caricature of his former self clad all in red: a physical manifestation of Luricawne as a **leprechaun**. He set up his lair in the center of town, which has become a dancefloor of madness and chaos.

If the characters arrive in Carlow after the Seanche, read or paraphrase the following:

> A distant rumble of dull thuds is heard in the distance. The sounds of the entire town dancing without music creates a cacophony of boots upon stone and shuffling of soles across rough ground and stone. The entire village is dancing in the center of the town. From a distance, a dwarf-sized, red-clad creature with exaggerated facial features sits on the edge of the fountain, waving the hammer in time with the dancing. "Come join us in a dance and accept some of the finest shoes you'll ever see. Our dancefloor always has space for more!"

After this welcome into the impromptu lair of the cursed Leath Brogan in his **leprechaun** form, and the battle begins. A successful DC 18 Sense Motive skill check alerts the characters that the dancers are unwilling participants; some are sobbing or crying, and others appear to be furious.

LEPRECHAUN   CR 2
XP 600
hp 18 (*Pathfinder Roleplaying Game Bestiary 2* "Leprechaun"

6. Wicklow

> A gentle breeze, the soothing crash of waves, and the smell of fried fish and potatoes are the first signs that a village is ahead. Coming up the rise of the next hill reveals a glimmering blue ocean and a quaint seaside town of clusters of stone buildings with slate rooves. The sails of small fishing vessels are clustered around the docks. In fact, much of the activity of this village is set around the docks, including a square with market stalls, a two-story tavern on the corner, and several fishmongers.

6-A. Fenlaugh Fish

This is a large rectangular building with double doors toward the docks for loading and processing fresh fish as they come off the boats. The fish is salted and preserved and sold fresh in a small storefront facing the square. Fineas Fenlaugh (*fin-ee-us fen-low*, N, male human, Cha 13; Exp 5; Profession [fisherman] +9) is the fifth Fenlaugh to run this business, and his family has worked for generations processing the fish that the locals harvest. He is to the town's center. He is a short man, barely crossing five feet, and is nearly as wide. One of the first things that people notice are his wide, thick-fingered hands crisscrossed with faint scars from years filleting fish. One can acquire a day's worth of salted fish for 4 cp.

6-B. The Smart Salmon

Bradan Feasa (*brothan fah-sa*), the Smart Salmon, was named in reference to the deeds of Finn mac Cumhaill (*Finn McCool*).

A weathered wooden sign depicts a salmon wearing glasses and reading a book. This tavern is well known for its fried fish, and the smell of crisp potatoes and breaded fish crisping in oil wafts through the whole village. The interior is crammed with bookshelves.

Anyone who visits the tavern leaves with the heavy smell of fried foods trapped in their clothing. The tavern is also known for serving citrusy white ale that pairs perfectly with the fresh fried cuts of fish. A plate and an ale costs 2 sp. **Grace** (CN, female human, Com 3; Cha 12; Intimidate +7), the barkeep, is a woman in her late 20s with a temper as fiery as it is fast. She's been known to snap at a drunken fool and shift to the sweetest and most inviting proprietress a moment later. She can often be heard arguing with her sister, Anne, whose own mercurial temper is more than a match for Grace's.

The Seanche in Wicklow

If the characters arrive before the Seanche, the town is exuberant, excited by the discovery of a silvery shoal of salmon.

The villagers are all busy working in the square, cleaning and filleting the catch before it is either salted or sent to the smokers. A small crowd of people is laughing and ending their labors as teenage boys and girls circulate among them with tankards of ale. As the local cats begin moving in, others rinse the square with buckets of saltwater and stiff-bristled brushes. The crowd drifts toward the tavern. The Seanche arrives in the early evening of the fifth night of the adventure as the party is really beginning in earnest. He enters the town playing his pipes, bringing music that seems to match and enhance the mood of this spontaneous celebration. He sings numerous songs of the sea, of loss, of treasures, or of fantastic creatures.

But the song he ends his night with tells a tale of a fisherman who murdered the wife of the King of Pikes. The King of Pikes then began sinking the ships from the fisherman's village, demanding that the fisherman give the king his wife. With a heavy heart, the village offered the fisherman's wife to the pike. At the last minute, the fisherman's wife turned to the pike and asked if he would not take her murderous husband instead. The pike did not have to think very long before it leapt from the water and snatched the fisherman up into its jaws before disappearing into the dark, choppy waters. With that, the Seanche retires to the stables for the evening and once again disappears early in the morning when the world is still waking or perhaps after the fishermen set out before the rest of the world rises.

A character may make a Knowledge (Arcana) check to discover what is happening. Consult the table below:

DC	Effect Noticed
10	There is something magical about this tune.
14	The effect is not influencing the people but it is drawing something from them.
18	The effect of the magic emanating from the lute and this man's voice is drawing some power or lifeforce in small portions from everyone in the crowd.

The music is not causing any lasting damage but anyone who fails a DC 15 Fortitude saving throw becomes exhausted.

The next day, the fishing fleet returns at midday in small groups. As they jockey into position and beginning mooring themselves, a shout goes up. A successful DC 22 Perception skill check allows a character to spot a long, large, dark shape in the waters below the ships. It looks to be about 10 feet long. In a splash of water and an explosion of wood, a giant pike crests the water and snatches one of the fishermen into its jaws before smashing its way through the ship and back into the dark, obscuring depths. The fishermen immediately abandon their ships by jumping from ship to ship until they reach shore.

The **giant pike** leaps across ships and attempts to grapple a creature and carry it into the water. The water below the ships and near the docks is only 30 feet deep at this time. The giant pike targets a fisherman or anyone who causes it harm. It attacks each round it can while maneuvering closer to the largest groups of prey. If it happens to devour a woman, it leaves, placated. While the pike attacks, the fishermen on the farthest ship set out frantically draw in their trawling net. The net is still spread from the ship to the ocean floor. Tangled in this net is the giant pike's wife, an equally enormous and thickly muscled giant pike. This pike snaps at anyone who approaches. If she is freed, both pikes join each other and leave the area.

Net: hardness 1; hp 20

GIANT PIKE (2) CR 4
XP 1,200
hp 39; (*Tome of Horrors Complete*, "Giant Pike")

The Emerald Plains

Before you is the aptly named Emerald Plains, a rich and rolling farmland filled with lush pastures, stands of tall straight trees, and crops neatly trimmed with tall hedges. To the northeast, Bru Na Brighid, Brighid's Tomb, can be seen, bearing its crafted stone bones to the sky as it rises from the underworld. To the south is Tabla An-Mohr, the Giant's Table, a plateau of pale gray stones. The top is stacked with piles of rock formations that create networks and pockets of caverns colloquially known as the Giant's Feast. Located directly to the east, a glimmering blue lake breaks the otherwise green rolling landscape. The Hartwood, the largest stand of trees in the plains, is directly west. Even from this distance, a glimmering silver tree can be seen standing far above the trees that surround it. To the north, the bountiful land breaks into a rocky shoreline of deep blue waters with several groups of buildings interspersed.

A successful DC 20 Perception skill check detects a glint of emerald among the rocks of the Giant's Table. At this point, it is advisable to share the area map with the characters. Allow them to see the various points of interest spread out on the map. The characters can explore the plains in any order they wish, but they inevitably encounter signs of the Seanche and the effects of his curse. Keep track of travel times because the timeline and path of the Seanche are denoted in the map and the characters may encounter him again. The Seanche's path leads to the center of the Hartwood where his final confrontation with Gnaddr occurs.

7. Tabla An-Mohr

The time of day drastically affects the appearance and environment of Tabla An-Mohr. During the nights or if the weather is extremely cold, very few signs of life can be found among the stacks of rocks on this windswept plateau. During the day, the area has traffic like that of a small city, albeit all of the travelers are various types of serpents. None of the serpents encountered is aggressive. The slopes of the plateau are steep inclines piled with loose shale and soil. Climbing the steep slope of the plateau can be completed with three consecutive successful DC 15 Climb skill checks. Fortunately, failure just results in an embarrassing and dusty slide to the bottom with boots full of dirt. If the characters fail and become frustrated, several local snakes notice their troubles and offer to assist them up the slope. These giant snakes allow the characters to cling to their tails.

7-A. The Giant's Feast Cave Formations

1. Rock Pile

This stack of rocks radiates the heat of the sun both day and night. A low and wide cavern entrance gapes like an open mouth into a 10-foot drop into a roughly circular 15-foot-wide chamber. The chamber is warm and dark but movement across the floor is immediately apparent even in the dark lighting. At night, 1d2+2 **venomous snake swarms** rest in the cavern. During the day, 1d3+1 **venomous snake swarms** are inside. In the midst of the snakes are three ornately decorated urns. The urns contain 161 gp, 317 sp, 339 sp, and a pair of silver raven earrings with topaz eyes.

VENOMOUS SNAKE SWARMS CR 4
XP 1,200
hp 37; *Pathfinder Roleplaying Game Bestiary 3* "Venomous Snake Swarm")

2. Cave Entrance

The entrance to this cavern system is tall and thin and requires a successful DC 15 Climb or Acrobatics check to traverse while wearing heavy armor. The cavern immediately begins to rise and widens against a rough cliff with numerous handholds available. The cliff rises 20 feet to a low and wide ledge that is about three feet high. It is possible to crawl forward to where the path branches into a fork, with the left path rising and the right path descending. The left path leads to a 15-foot-by-10-foot cave with a small opening onto a sunny ledge. This is the lair of several juvenile emerald nagas, and they are always present at night. There is a 3-in-10 chance that 2 **juvenile emerald nagas** (see **Appendix A**) are present during the day. Disturbing them alerts the other snakes in the area. The path to the right descends to a large 30-foot-by-20-foot rough-walled natural cavern. The floor is littered with bones, rusted weapons, worn equipment, and tattered clothing. Lounging about the cavern during the night are **10 venomous snakes**. During the day, only 5 **venomous snakes** are present.

VENOMOUS SNAKES (10) CR 1
XP 400
hp 13; (*Pathfinder Roleplaying Game Bestiary* "Venomous Snake")

GIANT'S FEAST
1 Square - 10 Feet
N
1
2
4
3

3. Cave

This cave has the most inviting entrance of all of the rock formations that make up the Giant's Feast. It can be seen from most of the plateau. A 30-foot-wide and 15-foot-tall entrance opens into an enormous cavern with a ceiling dotted with stalactites and a floor littered with stalagmites. A musky scent with hints of cloying sweetness accompanies the litter of snakeskins that fill the room. The only clear spot in the room is a bubbling pool that steams with heat. During the daytime, this room is empty. At night, 1d2+1 **venomous snake swarm** are here. The pool that warms the room is superheated by a **large fire elemental** trapped in a cold-iron cage. The cage is a six-inch ball of iron bands cut deeply with runes. It is cold to the touch despite being surrounded by the searing heat the angry elemental is pouring out. The fire elemental may escape its prison with a successful DC 19 *dispel magic* check. The fire elemental is quite upset about having been trapped and is immediately aggressive toward any nearby creatures.

VENOMOUS SNAKE SWARM   CR 4

XP 1,200

hp 37 (*Pathfinder Roleplaying Game Bestiary 3* "Venomous Snake Swarm")

FIRE ELEMENTAL, LARGE   CR 5

XP 1,600

hp 60 (*Pathfinder Roleplaying Game Bestiary* "Fire Elemental, Large"

4. The Main Dish

This rock formation dwarfs the other "dishes" present in the Giant's Feast and is clearly the main course. A wide cavern entrance shows that the cavern network immediately branches into three paths:

4a. This path wends itself around to the left for 35 feet before ending in a 10-foot-wide clearing. About 15 feet from the end of the passage, a crunching sound can be heard with each step, and snakeskins are piled several layers deep across the floor. At night, a **juvenile emerald naga** (see **Appendix A**) rests here. There is a 3-in-10 chance that it is present during daylight hours.

4b. This passage slopes gently downward for 40 feet before opening into a wide, low-ceilinged chamber with rough natural walls. Swinging a sword or melee weapon is difficult with the low ceiling, and anyone who is not wielding a piercing weapon such as a spear or a weapon with the *light* or *finesse* trait has disadvantage on attack rolls. Piles of coins and gems are strewn about the room, and careful observation detects emerald green scales among the piles. This chamber is the sleeping quarters of the **emerald naga queen** (see **Appendix A**).

4c. This narrow tunnel is about three feet wide and high, with a floor smoothed from regular travel. It stretches 15 feet before turning sharply to the right and continues for another 10 feet before opening into a roughly rectangular chamber 40 feet long by 30 feet wide. Interspersed along the sides of the cavern are eight 10-foot-wide pits in the floor.

Pit 1: Slowly pacing in the bottom of this pit is an elegantly dressed man who exudes fey charm (**summer knight**, see **Appendix A**). Despite being stuck in a pit, his fine clothing is spotless, and he appears relaxed. He addresses anyone who approaches the edge of the pit and looks at him. He demands to know what the characters are gawking at. He also informs them that despite being bored, he is not so bored that he would deign to speak with them. Of course, he continues to speak with the characters.

He has the following information that he imparts to those willing to listen to his egotistical conversation:

1. 1. This fey lord introduces himself as a knight of summer. He was sent by the Tuatha De Danann to return Gnaddr to his home plane. The emerald naga queen imprisoned him here.
2. 2. He is stuck in this realm until Gnaddr returns to his home plane; he is magically anchored to him.
3. 3. Of course he could escape if he wanted. The queen knows this, too. He says he told her that "he would not initiate an escape."
4. 4. The queen is a potential ally in stopping Gnaddr, but she is currently limited and bound by a deal she made with Gnaddr.
5. 5. A smith in the Lazy Lake may be willing to aid the characters if they attempt to stop Gnaddr.

> The man in the pit looks you over and says, "I have given the emerald queen my word that I will not leave here through my own power. But I have not given her my parole. I wish you well if you are trying to stop Gnaddr, and I would help you if I could."

A successful DC 15 Sense Motive skill check allows a character to discern the hints that the summer knight is dropping. He is able to aid the characters, but he is unable to affect his own escape or to assist in it.

Pit 2: This pit drops 20 feet and opens into a 30-foot-wide chamber. It contains a withered and long-dead body wrapped in the rotted clothes in which it expired. A beautiful gleaming shortsword still rests against the fingertips of the corpse, and several jeweled rings are on its bony fingers. The body is the mortal coil of an **ekimmu** (see **Appendix A**) trapped in this cell. Carefully examining the pit with a successful DC 20 Perception skill check allows a character to spot a thin rail of silver cut into the wall below the lip of the pit. The silver ribbon is scrawled with a script that does not seem to have a beginning or an end. The silver is evidence of ritual magic used to trap the ekimmu, and it blocks the ekimmu's Unnatural Aura from escaping the cell. The barrier that stops the ekimmu does not prevent a living being from entering or leaving. If the script is damaged or destroyed, the ekimmu is free and its Unnatural Aura immediately affects anyone in range. The ekimmu waits until the characters steal its former possessions before it materializes out of the body and surprises them with a Paralyzing Howl. The magical shortsword is named *Deadly Whisper* (see **Appendix B**), and the rings are worth 275 gp, 130 gp, and 35 gp.

Pit 3: This pit is a straight 20-foot drop, but after five feet nearly-clear crystals of ice coat the walls and floor to create a scintillating kaleidoscope of colors that is nearly mesmerizing. Any creature who descends more than five feet into the pit must make a DC 16 Fortitude saving throw. On a failed save, they take 3d6 points of cold damage. On a successful save, they take half this amount.

Pit 4: The interior of this 30-foot-deep pit appears to be constructed of rough tree bark, as though someone had turned a tree inside out. Small branches, unable to support significant weight, jut out of the sides with regularity. The bottom of the pit is filled with a pale jade green liquid. A creature who touches the liquid must make a DC 16 Fortitude saving throw. On a failed saving throw, its movement is halved as the creature begin to grow bark. The creature must make another saving throw at the beginning of its next turn. A creature who fails three saves becomes a petrified statue of bark for 24 hours. A creature who succeeds on any of the saving throws ends the effects and is immune to the liquid for 24 hours.

Pit 5: The interior of this 20-foot-deep pit is coated with iron plates riveted to the floor and walls. The walls of this pit are coated with an enchanted cold iron that deals 1d4 points of Constitution damage to any that touches it. A five-foot wooden dais rises from the center. An ornate wooden chair with a back splat limned with leaf-like carvings continues into relief carvings that extend down the legs into ball and claw feet. The wood itself is a rich red mahogany seemingly flecked with gold. The chair has been polished into a high glossy sheen.

Pit 6: This pit descends six feet to a dark liquid pool as still as glass. Despite the thirst for light this liquid exhibits, intelligent creatures are reflected in the pool. Anyone touching the liquid must make a DC 16 Will saving throw. On a failed save, the liquid begins to coat their body wherever they touched it and they suffer 1d4 points of Intelligence damage and the creature is pinned. On a successful save, they suffer half this damage and are not pinned. A pinned creature takes 1d4 points of Intelligence damage at the end of each of its turns. The creature can remove the pinned condition with a successful combat maneuver check or Escape Artist skill check against DC 16.

Pit 7: This pit is only 10 feet deep, and the walls and floor are covered in irregular rock formations. Anyone observing the rock for 12 or more seconds may make a successful DC 15 Perception skill check to notice that the rock here is moving slightly, perhaps as if it is breathing. If loud noises are made or if the rock floor or walls are touched, a single saucer-sized eye slowly opens and observes the area. This creature is an **elemental adder** (see **Appendix A**) of rock. Q'rack, the elemental adder, attacks anyone attempting to free a prisoner. He does not do anything if the ekimmu is disturbed. He is the guardian of the cells. As long as the characters have SS'Thissk's permission, he does not disturb them as they explore this area.

Pit 8: This 15-foot-deep pit has a bare stone floor and walls covered in what seems to be thousands of skulls. With a successful DC 15 Heal skill check, a character can determine that these skulls range in age from several months to hundreds of years. The species of the skulls is quite diverse and ranges from beast to humanoid, including a cyclops, several with lizard or draconic features, and creatures with canine and feline features. The skulls react whenever they see an intelligent creature (they have a +6 Perception). If they notice anyone, a great number of them begin attempting to speak to the closest creature in a variety of languages. To filter out the cacophony and to cast a spell or to listen to a single skull requires a successful DC 14 concentration check. A failure means that this character cannot identify a single voice and may not cast any spell that has a verbal component. The skulls do not stop speaking until they do not detect anyone. A creature that ends its turn within five feet of the skulls when inside the pit provokes 1d6 Skull Wall Bite attacks, which have a +8 melee attack bonus and deal 2d6 +4 points of damage on a successful hit.

7-B. The Queen of the Emerald Serpents

During the day, SS'Thissk, an **emerald naga queen** (see **Appendix A**), lounges upon the tallest piles of rocks on the plateau. She enjoys the heat of the sun and the expansive view of the lands around her. Her body scintillates with hues of green and casts strange, liquid-like shadows that ripple and move. Her coiled body seems to stretch 20 feet and ends in a perfectly shaped and comely green-skinned humanoid face. She wears a simple, supple, honey-brown leather halter with several small pouches. She always rests alongside or atop 2 **constrictor snakes** that accompany her everywhere she goes. There are also 3 **juvenile emerald nagas** (see **Appendix A**) nearby enjoying the sun shining on their sparkling green scales. If SS'Thissk is approached in a friendly manner — perhaps with a gift recognizing her authority as the queen of the emerald serpents, her preferred title, — she listens and shares information. It benefits her if the characters deal with Gnaddr because it frees her of the *geased* deal that traps her and her family on this plane. She desires nothing more than to return home, especially with the treasure she thought she had tricked from Gnaddr. If the characters persuade her to help, they may gain some assistance. What she provides depends upon the degree of success the characters achieve with a Diplomacy skill check, treating her attitude as being indifferent.

DC	Boon
14	*Potion of cure moderate wounds*
19	*Restorative ointment*
24	*Potion of cure critical wounds*

The queen shares the following information with the characters:
- Gnaddr and his minions are vulnerable to weapons wrought from the cold iron obtained from a fallen star.
- Although he may seem alone, Gnaddr always has a retinue of creatures protecting him. The queen has seen him most often with a pack of wolf-like creatures from his home plane. These creatures heal themselves if they aren't silenced.
- The Lazy Lake is known for its puissant arms. If asked to elaborate, the queen seems surprised that the characters haven't found arms in lakes before.

CONSTRICTOR SNAKE (2)　　　　　**CR 2**
XP 400
hp 19; (*Pathfinder Roleplaying Game Bestiary* "Constrictor Snake")

8. Bru Na Brighid

A round-topped hill obscures a view of the sea behind it. Its waist is covered in lush green grass, and a stone structure emerges from the rich soil. The structure is built from large, roughly worked stones, and several entrances lead into it from each cardinal direction. Several small buildings are built around the base of the wide low hill, and people can be seen moving about from a distance. If the hill is observed for most of a day, people are likely observed climbing up and into the structure.

An inn with a tavern, a general goods store, and several homes are clustered near a path leading to the top of the hill. The path is well worn and clearly maintained. Neat lines of rocks mark the edges and the beginning of the path. Candles are placed upon flattish stones every six to 10 feet and on some evenings they are lit, wending a twinkling path to the shrine that rises from the hill.

When the characters enter the village, a commotion can be heard with a successful DC 10 Perception skill check. Snakes cover the ground outside the window and around the buildings and on the road. The small snakes swarming the ground are not the most disturbing thing, however; that would be the brightly glimmering emerald snake stretching more than 10 feet long with an exquisite woman's face. She is followed by three smaller yet similar snake creatures with the faces of teenage girls. This group of serpents consists of an **emerald naga** (see **Appendix A**), 3 **juvenile emerald nagas** (see **Appendix A**), and 5 **venomous snakes**. They are moving through the village, with some of the smaller snakes eating and killing small, domesticated animals. A character who succeeds on a DC 15 Sense Motive skill check notices that the nagas seem to be herding the snakes and attempting to move them through the village as quickly as possible. If the nagas are unmolested, they respectfully nod to the characters and continue herding the snakes away from the cluster of buildings as quickly as they can. If the characters engage the nagas in an aggressive manner, the emerald naga and one of the juvenile emerald nagas attempt to keep the characters busy while the rest of the serpents escape toward Tabla An-Mohr. The characters also suffer a –2 circumstance penalty on their first Diplomacy skill check with the emerald naga queen.

However the interaction with the nagas goes, the villagers are grateful for the characters' intervention.

VENOMOUS SNAKES (5)　CR 1
XP 400
hp 13; (*Pathfinder Roleplaying Game Bestiary* "Venomous Snake")

8-A. Brighid's Rest

This inn has a stable, six guest rooms, and a cozy tavern that serves flavorful and hearty local cuisine. **Roisin** (*ro-sheen*, N, female human Com 3; Cha 12; Profession [barkeeper] +6) runs this tavern with her two teenage boys. Her husband "run off with some trollop years ago." She provides quality service in a clean tavern. She provides a mug of ale and a bowl of stew or shepherd's pie for 6 cp. A heartier spread can be had for 1 sp. She also offers several local ales ranging in quality and price from 1 cp to 1 sp. Her sons **Oisin** (*O-sheen*) and **Darragh** (*Darra*, N, male humans Com 2; Str 12; Climb +5) are hardworking and jovial boys. They are quick to help and just as quick to get into some trouble if they aren't busy. They are often found in the stable playing dice and sipping pilfered ale.

8-B. Senan's Sundry Shop

Senan's shop is housed in a sunflower tallow building with fading blue shutters and a blue door faded at the bottom from years of weather and use. A small brass bell jingles noisily when the door is opened to reveal a shelf-filled room lined with a cluttered countertop. The plethora of items jammed into this store masks the truly useful items. Any mundane equipment can be found here if a character makes a successful DC 12 Perception skill check. **Ronan McFarren** (CN, male human Exp 4; Cha 14; Diplomacy +7) is a wiry gentleman wearing a leather apron with pockets stuffed with a variety of tools and trinkets. He is friendly and tries to be helpful, but he is not completely sure what he has in the shop. He purchased the shop from Senan Walsh III, whose family owned the shop for three generations.

Ronan has been attempting to court Roisin for several years. He can be found drinking at the tavern or helping the boys with some repair tasks when he isn't in his shop or the apartment above it. Much of his business is in the sale of sacred stones marked with a single rune that are said to grant wishes if dropped into Brighid's Throat within the structure atop the hill. Ronan sells these for 5 cp. He also has several interesting rumors about the area that can be worked into any roleplaying interaction:

- Brighid rode across the sea on a great fiery stallion and collapsed on the hill in a smoldering fire, laying her armor and spear beside her on the stones. She rested on the rocks and entered a shimmering portal the next day dressed in a diaphanous golden gown that floated about her.
- The best fried fish can be found nearby in the village of Wicklow at the Smart Salmon.
- A sea monster has been wrecking all the nets along the coast.

The Seanche in Bru Na Brighid

If the characters arrive during the Seanche's visit to the village (which occurs on the sixth day and seventh night of the adventure), they may see the following:

When the Seanche arrives, he heads to the tavern, as usual. He converses briefly with Roisin and then sets up in a corner near the fire. He chats and spreads local rumors and knowledge and then begins playing. He takes requests for several hours before beginning his cursed song.

The Seanche begins playing a haunting and rhythmic tune, and the room begins to hush. He tells a story about a farmer finding a wrinkled old man in a green vest walking with a shovel on the edge of his property. The little fey man was startled by the farmer, who captured him. The little fey man offered the farmer a deal: If the farmer freed him, he would show him where he buried his gold treasure. The farmer eagerly agreed and found the treasure. He then freed the little fey man and kicked him off his property. The farmer's family became wealthy but were cursed with small annoyances and misfortunes.

The song ends and the crowd appears exhausted as they filter out into the night. The Seanche retires to the stables for the night.

A character may make a Knowledge (Arcana) skill check to discover what is happening. Consult the table below:

DC	Effect Noticed
10	There is something magical about this tune.
15	The effect is not influencing the people but it is drawing something from them.
20	The effect of the magic emanating from the lute and this man's voice is drawing some power or lifeforce in small portions from everyone in the crowd.

The music is not causing any lasting damage but anyone who fails a DC 15 Fortitude saving throw becomes exhausted.

The next day, Ronan and the boys capture a tiny old man in a barrel that they bring into Brighid's Rest. They demand gold from the creature, and poke it with sticks and threaten it.

"Fine, I'll give ye what ye want," a tinny voice rasps from the barrel.

The boys stop poking with their sticks, and Ronan reaches into the barrel. He pulls a foot-and-a-half tall figure clad in roughspun brown woolen clothes and shod in brown shoes with burnished gold buckles.

"You swear?" Ronan demands.

"I swear I will take you to the spot I buried those coins but ye don't want them. They're cursed," the little man squeaks seriously.

Ronan plops him onto the ground unceremoniously, and the little man dusts himself off, throwing an angry glare at Ronan. He begins heading just outside of town and into a copse of trees. There, Ronan and the boys dig up an iron cauldron with wooden and leather handles.

The boys and Ronan take the pot to Brighid's Rest and open it to reveal a mound of 50 saucer-sized golden coins. The coins immediately sprout wings and scatter throughout the building and hide until they can make their way back to their true owner. The *leprechaun's gold* (see **Appendix B**) can be found around the area until all 50 coins are discovered or until two weeks pass.

8-C. Brighid's Shrine

The worn path leads to the summit of the hill and the stone shrine emerging from it, where it splits to circle the entire summit. At the summit, pea-sized gravel replaces the path. Four entrances lead into the shrine, with one facing each cardinal direction. Another level of dirt and a stone structure rises above the entrance level.

1. Main Chamber

The main chamber of this structure is 100 feet across and roughly circular. The walls are stone and packed dirt. A staircase cut into the wall along the northwestern wall rises up to the ceiling. A 10-foot-wide pit in the center of the shrine falls into a dark chamber. The floor around the pit is worn from years of traffic. A golden statue of Brighid and a golden steed hangs on finely wrought brass chains above the pit, affording clear views of it from up and down the shaft. The wooden statue is covered in gold leaf and is worth 225 gp. However, anyone taking the statue is cursed until they complete three long rests. A cursed creature who rolls a natural 20 on an attack roll, skill check, or saving throw must reroll and use the second result.

2. Treasure Pit

The pit drops onto a pile of small stones in the center of a pool of water. Three islands appear to be empty rises of smooth stone. Crude carvings of boars, sheep, and figures working forges decorate the walls. Each of the islands has a roughly circular spot near the center that is polished and limned in carefully etched glyphs. A successful DC 15 Knowledge (Arcana or Religion) skill check allows the characters to discern several of the glyphs and their meaning. The words "light," "protect," "reveal," and "flames" are repeated in each circle. The glyphs of each circle are identical. If the brass shield (**Area 3**) above the pit is polished, light reflected from it strikes the stones and the water below and scatters throughout the entire room to create a bright light that reveals three chests, one in the center of each circle.

One chest contains a bronze spearhead nicked from battle; it awaits only being attached to once again see battle. One chest holds a bronze breastplate that gleams like gold in the sunlight. The final chest contains a much nicer version of the shield that hangs above the shaft. This shield gleams and when lifted, two soft leather bags are found below that contain a figurine of a boar and a ram. See **Appendix B** for *Brighid's raiment and arms*.

3. Upper Chamber

Stairs lead into a narrow and winding passage that rises clockwise to a small chamber built from four wide stone plinths oriented along the cardinal directions. A five-foot-diameter pit in the floor is directly above the pit in the room below. Thin spaces exist in the corners, and a character who is small, unarmored, or lightly armored could squeeze through with a successful DC 15 Escape Artist skill check. Mounted into the stone ceiling above the pit is a bronze shield depicting a rising sun. The shield's age is marked with verdigris that gives it a bluish-green hue that nearly matches the sea outside. The shield can be removed from its clips with a little bit of time and elbow grease. If it is polished, it reflects sunlight down into the pit and causes the chests to appear in the treasure pit (**Area 2**).

BRIGHID

In Celtic mythology, Brighid or Brig, is the goddess of spring, health and healing, poetry, fertility, and smithing. She is a member of the Tuatha De Danann and is the daughter of the Dagda, the "father" of Celtic gods. Her feast day is traditionally February 1st and 2nd, which was a pagan festival called Imbolc.

Brighid's temples and shrines are always represented by an eternal flame tended by her priestesses, the Fire Keepers. Her temples and sanctums often contain tools she leaves for the mortals she loves and protects.

Farmers, smiths, soldiers, and other common folk often worship Brighid. Many tales speak of her fearsome and fiery protection touching and affecting the lives of those who worship her.

Suggested Domains: Artifice, Good, Sun

Tenets: To protect the family and children. To protect order and peace. To support community.

9. THE LAZY LAKE

The blue waters of this lake slap choppily against the lightly wooded shoreline. The lake spreads in a kidney shape several thousand feet across and wide. The water is cool, dark, and fresh.

Searching the shore of the lake with a successful DC 16 Perception skill check reveals several popular fishing spots and a few tree stands for bowhunting. The tree stands provide partial cover to anyone inside against attacks emanating from outside the tree stands. A rocky isle covered in dense, scraggly pines juts from the rough waters near the center of the lake. Getting to the island can be challenging. There are no convenient boats, but a great deal of fallen and fresh trees could easily be fashioned into a raft. The waters of the lake are choppy during the day due to the 14 **each-uisces** (*ahk ish keh*, see **Appendix A**) that spend their days playing and running through the waters, creating tumultuous and unpredictable currents. These energetic water horses are playful, which can appear aggressive. They attempt to capsize any vessel that enters the waters so that they may swim and play with the creatures attempting to cross. If a creature truly appears in distress, they bring them to shore. To calm an each-uisce, a character can attempt to gain its attention and favor. This can be done with food or gentle approaches and if the character succeeds on a Diplomacy skill check treating the each-uisces' starting attitude as friendly. After this, the each-uisce follows simple commands and transports the character to the island. If attacked, they fight for a few rounds before retreating. They immediately swim away if any of them are killed.

The shores of the isle are quite rocky and irregular, creating numerous small pools and crevasses ideal for hiding abundant life. Thick pines ring the entire isle, and their scratchy needles and sharp branches cause 1d4 points of damage to anyone who simply pushes through them. Moving through at a more cautious pace and cutting branches or using magic makes this task much safer. If magic is used, remember that although these are pine trees, they are fresh and somewhat resistant to bursting into flames. Characters must push through the trees for about 25 feet until they find a clearing with a spring forming a wide, clear pool.

Characters who make a DC 20 Perception skill check notice a ripple recurring in the center of the pool at regular intervals, and they even hear a dull thud and see a muscular woman swinging a hammer at a red and yellow glowing piece of metal. She looks up and notices the characters observing her. She lifts a hand and waves them down toward her. The water in the pool is warm, like bathwater, but only five feet deep. A slightly resistant dome of air forms underwater around the forge and the smith. Crossing into the dome is difficult terrain and anyone entering from the top falls 10 feet to the stone ground of this underwater forge and may take damage. Fish, the each-uisce, and other aquatic animals swim around this dome of air. The smith refuses to help the characters if they killed any each-uisce.

The forge itself appears to be a well with a metal liner and rim filled with flowing hot magma. Occasionally, the smith dips her sword into the magma, pounds determinedly, and then plunges it into the water that makes up the walls around her forge. The air is humid and smells of old eggs and soot. She places the piece she is working with on a steel bench.

"Greetings! I am the lady of this lake. The land tells me you have dire need." The smith speaks with a rich and melodious voice that carries over the sizzling of heat and water. "If you assist me, I can arm you with the power of this land. This lake was created by a lazy faerie who was busy cavorting with humans rather than maintaining the spring here. Well, a piece of falling iron struck and killed her lover at this very lake. We have time enough to build you a weapon. What is it we should make? A sword? Yes, that will do. What we need to do is this …"

The smith explains the steps of the process and what she needs:

1. "BRING ME THE METAL."

A character must retrieve the meteoric iron from the nearby depression. Unfortunately, the each-uisce love a good game of keep away. They attempt to knock the ore from a character's hands and pass it to each other. The character needs to succeed at two consecutive grapple checks to avoid the water horses to get the ore to the bubble, even though the character is not actually trying to grapple them.

2. "HELP ME SMELT THE ORE."

Characters must place the iron into the crucible and lower it into the magma until the ore glows a bluish-white. The smith uses a bellows on the magma while she intensely concentrates on the ore. She signals the characters when to remove it.

This requires two characters to lift the bars on each side of the crucible and lower it into the magma to melt. Two consecutive successful DC 15 Strength checks are needed to successfully melt the ore. Both characters involved suffer 1d4 points of fire damage from the heat of the magma. If one or both of them fails or if the two checks differ by more than 5, the crucible falls and spills the heated ore dealing 4d6 points of damage, though a successful DC 15 Reflex saving halves the fire damage.

3. "HELP ME POUR THE ORE."

Characters must help pour the ore into the mold and safely return the crucible to its cradle while the smith carefully crumbles a glittering whitish powder into the mold.

This portion of the task requires a more delicate hand. To pour the molten ore requires a successful DC 15 Sleight of Hand skill check to add the ore while the smith crumbles some powder into the mold. On a failure, a character takes 4d6 points of fire damage, though a successful DC 15 Reflex saving throw halves the damage.

4. "HELP ME SHATTER THE MOLD."

Despite how it sounds, shattering the mold actually requires someone to examine the mold and determine the correct spot to strike it. A character who examines the mold with a successful DC 15 Disable Device check identifies the single correct spot to strike the mold to free the gleaming bluish blade. A character must hold a cold chisel while the smith strikes with the hammer. If they select the incorrect spot, the sword shatters, forcing all creatures within the air bubble to make a DC 15 Reflex saving throw. A creature that fails takes 3d6 points of damage while one who succeeds takes half this amount.

The players are rewarded for their efforts with the *feyslayer sword* (see **Appendix B**), which can be any type of sword chosen by the characters, though a longsword is the default variety.

10. The Hartwood

The thick boles create a wall that prevents easy entry into this dark forest. The only visible path is a dark arched tunnel of tree branches over a partially overgrown trail. A yellow and green pavilion tent sits in a grassy area to the side of the road before the forest. It protects a tidy firepit and a wooden plank table covered in white linen and set with silver serving dishes and ewers. Several horses are tethered nearby, and a group of four armored figures with green and gold tabards are completing various chores around the camp. A reed-thin woman with pale jade skin and almond-shaped golden eyes stands nearby. She is clad in scale mail so green it is nearly black. She holds a silver-bladed glaive with a handle of polished ebony. A pair of hand crossbows hang from her belt next to a longsword with a silver pommel and a handle wrapped in black leather.

If the characters approach the woods, one of Lady Puinseann's men (4 **steel elves**, see **Appendix A**) approaches with his hands held palm forward to invite the characters to join his lady for a drink and brief repast. If they refuse, he calmly returns to his lady and quietly informs her of the characters' decision. At this, **Lady Puinseann** (see **Appendix A**) drains her goblet of wine, picks up her glaive, and goes to meet the party in battle in the road with her warriors. Her strategy is to disable any spellcasters while her foot soldiers tie up the melee fighters. Whether or not Gnaddr or the Seanche have arrived, Lady Puinseann attempts to prevent the characters from entering the forest. If they sneak past her, they encounter 12 **fey lupes** (see **Appendix A**) and she and her troops join the fight in an attempt to drive the characters away. She even accepts surrender or ceasefire if that becomes an option.

If the characters join her, read or paraphrase the following:

"I am Lady Puinseann. What is your business in these woods?"

She motions for you to join her at the table, and one of her soldiers pours wine and offers platters of food. Once you are served, she says, "I offer you this repast with no obligations or ill intentions."

She refills her wine goblet and motions for you to join her in a toast, "To good health and fortunes."

Lady Puinseann attempts to dissuade the characters from entering the woods and interfering with Gnaddr's plans. If they seem insistent, she offers them several items to abandon their plans and leave the Hartwood. She offers a set of *elven chain*, a *mantle of spell resistance*, and a perfect diamond worth 1,000 gp.

If the characters refuse, she sighs and scans the characters with a resigned look. Read the following:

"Are you sure?" As she speaks, she takes her longspear in her hand and casually moves away from the table and camp. "Whenever you are ready," the lady says with a disappointed look and a nod to her troops.

Combat begins as if the characters had refused her meal as described above.

10-1. Traveling in the Hartwood

While traveling in the Hartwood, it is an easy task to stay on the path that leads to the Eo Mughna. If the characters venture off the path, they have a 3-in-6 chance of an encounter for each hour of travel.

Hartwood Random Encounters

1d4	Encounter
1	6 fey lupes (see **Appendix A**)
2	1d3 **army ant swarms**
3	White stag (as **deer**)
4	10 **fey lupes** (see **Appendix A**)

10-2. Eo Mughna

At the center of the Hartwood stands Eo Mughna, the Mighty Yew, which is actually a magnificent oak tree with a bark that shimmers with a glint of silver and gold. Although it stands only about 50 feet tall, it dwarfs the smaller trees around it. A character who makes a successful DC 15 Perception skill check determines that the upper branches of the tree are laden with apples, hazelnuts, and acorns. The bark is flecked with tiny motes of silver and gold.

Seanche's Lament

The Seanche's goal is to finish the song he has been cursed to play, while Gnaddr's goal is to kill and sacrifice the willing Seanche in order to open the gates and release his army. The timeline of the Seanche allows for three potential outcomes in the Hartwood at the Eo Mughna:

1. The Characters Arrive First

If the characters arrive before the Seanche, they find **Gnaddr** (see **Appendix A**) waiting at the tree. He greets the characters cordially, as if they were expected. Hidden in the woods are 8 **fey lupes** (see **Appendix A**) that can be spotted with a successful DC 18 Perception skill check.

> "Ah. You've come to witness the arrival and to hear the dreadful bard's last lament? Find a spot to observe. Unless … oh yes, that's it, you've come to interfere."

At this exact moment, the fey lupes make a surprise attack on the characters, and the battle with Gnaddr begins in earnest.

2. The Characters Arrive with the Seanche

The characters arriving with the Seanche is the most disruptive outcome for Gnaddr's plans, and he immediately uses the *suggestion* spell to cause the Seanche to begin playing the cursed lute. Gnaddr's first attack on his first round is made with the silvered knife against the Eo Mughna. This causes the tree to bleed sap, and a glimmering thread forms between the Seanche and the Eo Mughna. This connection remains for as long as the Seanche continues to play. On the second round, the Seanche loses a hit die and a low mist rolls in from the forest. When the Seanche loses 4 Hit Dice, the 12 **fey lupes** arrive out of the mist to aid Gnaddr if they have not already been killed. When the Seanche has no more Hit Dice remaining, the misty bridge forms and Gnaddr's army is unstoppable.

3. The Seanche Arrives Before the Characters

If the Seanche arrives before the characters, Gnaddr's lieutenant and her troops escort him to the Eo Mughna if they are still able. Otherwise, the Seanche makes his way through the Hartwood, counting on the *pass without trace* effect of the cursed lute to keep him safe. When he arrives, Gnaddr is casually leaning against the Eo Mughna and idly toying with a silver dagger. Once the Seanche enters the clearing, the 12 **fey lupes** (see **Appendix A**) slip through the trees in an ever-tightening circle. They remain outside the clearing until an unspoken signal from Gnaddr summons them to action. Gnaddr uses *suggestion* to have the Seanche play the cursed lute and begin opening the bridge of mists. For each day the characters are behind the Seanche's arrival, he loses a hit die. If he has already lost 4 Hit Dice when the characters arrive, the 12 **fey lupes** are baying at the Seanche's feet.

Conclusion

If the ritual is stopped, the *uillean pipes of reality* shatter, lifting the Seanche's curse and causing Gnaddr, or his body, to be pulled into the mist by large dark shapes as snow begins to fall. After he is dragged into the mist, the *torc na goineog* (see **Appendix B**) is tossed into the clearing and lands in front of the Eo Mughna.

The emerald naga queen (see **Appendix A**) arrives a short time later with all of her retinue; so many snakes arrive that they seem to carpet her forest. She thanks the characters for retrieving the *torc na goineog* for her. If the characters attempt to stop the emerald naga queen from taking the torc, she and her snakes attack. She has 6 **emerald nagas** (see **Appendix A**), 10 **juvenile emerald nagas** (see **Appendix A**), and 5 **venomous snake swarms** with her. As the snakes make their way past the Eo Mughna and into the mist, a small wooden chest is left in front of the characters. The chest contains three golden statuettes of snakes with emerald eyes. Each statuette is wrapped in velvet. The statues are worth 740 gp each and measure about a foot tall. The people of this region tell the tale of the snakes leaving their land for many years to come, often conflating the story with the chaos the Seanche sowed and even acknowledging him as driving the snakes from the land.

The following NPCs and new monsters are found in *The Seanche's Lament*.

BEAN FIONN

A drowning sidhe is created when a fey creature fails in its vow to protect a body of water. The effects of this failure create a variety of drastic changes in a landscape: a lake goes dry, a small brook becomes a lake, a mountain spring becomes a raging waterfall, etc. The drowning sidhe, who is still bound to the area they failed to protect, transforms into a perversion of its former self, often re-enacting the very event that caused their failure. Although intelligent and still beautiful, they are volatile and unpredictable.

BEAN FIONN   CR 2

XP 600
CN Medium fey (aquatic)
Init +3; **Senses** low-light vision; **Perception** +3

AC 13, touch 11, flat-footed 12 (+1 Dex, +2 natural)
hp 22 (4d6+8)
Fort +3; **Ref** +7; **Will** +3
Immune sleep; **Resist** cold 5

Speed 30 ft., swim 30 ft.
Melee headbutt +2 (1d3)
Special Attacks beguiling kiss, drowning tide, 3/day (20–ft. cone, DC 14 half, 2d6 cold)

Abilities Str 11, Dex 16, Con 15, Int 17, Wis 8, Cha 8
Base Atk +2; **CMB** +2 (+4 grapple); **CMD** 15 (17 vs. grapple)
Feats Improved Grapple, Improved Unarmed Strike
Skills Bluff +6, Diplomacy +6, Disguise +5, Escape Artist +10, Perception +6, Sense Motive +6, Sleight of Hand +10, Stealth +9, Swim +16
Languages Common, Sylvan

Beguiling Kiss (Su) A bean fionn charms creatures it can cajole into kissing it. An unwilling victim must be grappled before the bean fionn can use this ability. The bean fionn's kiss deals 1d3 Wisdom damage. The kiss also has the effect of a *charm person* spell. The victim must succeed on a DC 11 Will save to negate the *charm person*. The save DC is Charisma-based.

Drowning Tide (Su) Three times per day as a standard action, a bean fionn can release a blast of freezing mist in a 20–ft. cone. A creature in the area takes 2d6 points of cold damage (DC 14 Reflex for half). The save DC is Constitution-based.

DOIRCHE

A wild eyed greasy face pokes through a mane of unkempt hair and scraggly beard. The man wears rough hide armor and carries a bone rattle and a silver sickle. His filthy hands are caked in dirt and dried blood. A nearly toothless mouth smacks wetly as he eyes you ravenously.

DOIRCHE   CR 6

XP 2,400
CN Medium fey
Init +7; **Senses** low-light vision; **Perception** +13

AC 16, touch 12, flat-footed 14 (+4 armor, +2 Dex)
hp 60 (8d6+32)
Fort +6; **Ref** +8; **Will** +7
DR 10/magic; **Immune** mind-affecting effects; **Resist** electricity 10

Speed 30 ft.
Melee 2 silver sickles +8 (1d6+4)
Special Attacks
Spells Prepared (CL 7th; concentration +13)
4th — *chaos hammer* (DC 18), *poison* (DC 18)
3rd — *bestow curse, deeper darkness, magic circle against law* (DC 17)
2nd — *align weapon (chaos only), hold person* (DC 16), *sound burst, spiritual weapon*
1st — *bless water, divine favor, inflict light wounds, protection from law, shield of faith*
0 (at will) — *detect magic, guidance, read magic, stabilize*

Abilities Str 14, Dex 15, Con 18, Int 12, Wis 18, Cha 10
Base Atk +4; **CMB** +6; **CMD** 18
Feats Cleave, Improved Initiative, Power Attack, Weapon Focus (sickle)
Skills Acrobatics +11, Bluff +9, Climb +11, Escape Artist +11, Intimidate +6, Knowledge (nature) +10, Perception +13, Sense Motive +15, Stealth +15
Languages Common, Sylvan
SQ mysterious smoke

Mysterious Smoke (Su) Once every 1d4 rounds as a swift action, the doirche can instantly teleport to a location it can see within 50 feet of it. When it does so, it leaves a 10-ft. high, 5-ft. diameter cylinder of wispy smoke where it previously stood. The smoke duplicates the effects of an *obscuring mist* spell.
Spells The doirche casts spells as a 7th-level cleric.

EACH-UISCE

These playful and energetic creatures seem to be made completely of water but they hold the clear form of a horse. They are often found in herds and with or near intelligent species with which they may work.

EACH-UISCE   CR 1

XP 400
CN Large fey (aquatic)
Init +3; **Senses** low-light vision; **Perception** +6

AC 11, touch 11, flat-footed 9 (+2 Dex, −1 size)
hp 15 (2d6+8)
Fort +4; **Ref** +5; **Will** +4
DR 5/cold iron; **SR** 12

Speed 20 ft., swim 30 ft.
Melee slam +5 (1d6 +3 plus grab)
Space 10 ft.; **Reach** 10 ft

Abilities Str 17, Dex 14, Con 18, Int 12, Wis 13, Cha 7
Base Atk +1; **CMB** +5; **CMD** 17
Feats Weapon Focus (unarmed strike)
Skills Bluff +3, Craft (alchemy) +5, Escape Artist +8, Handle Animal +0, Perception +6, Perform (dance) +2, Sense Motive +5, Stealth +12, Swim +10
Languages understands Sylvan but cannot speak

Ekimmu

Ekimmu are the spirits of the dead who have not been given proper funerary rites. They may be murder victims cast into a defile, lonely hermits who died far away from others, or travelers too far from home for anyone to claim their corpses. Denied entry into the afterlife, they roam the world looking to vent their wrath upon mortals. They often do this by possessing a person and committing violent crimes, abandoning their victim when suspicions are aroused. Some legends say that an ekimmu can be quieted or even laid to rest if invited to a funerary feast and offered the appropriate libations.

Ekimmu   CR 5

XP 1,600
CE Medium undead (incorporeal)
Init +7; **Senses** darkvision 60 ft.; **Perception** +10
Aura unnatural aura (30 ft.)

AC 18, touch 18, flat-footed 14 (+5 deflection, +3 Dex)
hp 47 (5d8+25)
Fort +6; **Ref** +4; **Will** +6
Defensive Abilities channel resistance +2, incorporeal;
Immune undead traits

Speed fly 60 ft. (good)
Melee incorporeal touch +5 (2d6 negative energy)
Special Attacks paralyzing howl 1/day
Spell-Like Abilities (CL 10th)
1/day—*magic jar*

Abilities Str –, Dex 16, Con –, Int 14, Wis 14, Cha 21
Base Atk +3; **CMB** +6; **CMD** 16
Feats Blind-Fight, Combat Reflexes, Improved Initiative
Skills Bluff +3, Craft (alchemy) +5, Escape Artist +8, Handle Animal +0, Perception +6, Perform (dance) +2, Sense Motive +5, Stealth +12, Swim +10
Languages any languages it knew in life

Paralyzing Howl (Su) The ekimmu can howl three times per day as a standard action. This howl is a sonic effect that fills a 30-foot radius burst, centered on the ekimmu. Any non-undead caught within this area must succeed on a DC 17 Will save or be paralyzed for 1d4 rounds. This is a mind-affecting fear effect in addition to a sonic effect. The save DC is Charisma-based.

Elemental Adder

An elemental adder is a snake made up of the elements of its home plane. This particular entry covers the elemental adder from the Plane of Earth, but they can easily be found on any elemental plane. These creatures are much more intelligent than many are wont to believe, and rumors even exist of ancient and powerful elemental adders who have mastered the arcane arts.

Elemental Adder   CR 8

XP 4,800
N Large fey
Init +8; **Senses** low-light vision, tremorsense 60 ft.; **Perception** +20

AC 18, touch 12, flat-footed 16 (+1 Dex, +1 dodge, +7 natural, –1 size)
hp 97 (13d6+52)
Fort +8; **Ref** +9; **Will** +10
DR 10/magic; **Immune** mind-affecting effects

Speed 40 ft.
Melee bite +12 (2d6+6 plus poison), tail +9 (2d6+2)
Space 10 ft.; **Reach** 10 ft.
Special Attacks constrict (tail, 2d6+9), phase strike
Spells Known (CL 9th; concentration +13)
4th (5/day)— *charm monster* (DC 18), *phantasmal killer* (DC 18)
3rd (7/day)— *dispel magic, fireball, suggestion* (DC 17)
2nd (7/day) — *blur, hold person* (DC 16), *invisibility, scorching ray*
1st (7/day)— *charm person* (DC 15), *color spray, fog cloud, mage armor, magic missile*
0 (at will)—*daze* (DC 14), *detect magic, flare* (DC 14), *mage hand, message, open/close, read magic, touch of fatigue*

Abilities Str 20, Dex 12, Con 18, Int 9, Wis 10, Cha 6
Base Atk +6; **CMB** +12; **CMD** 24
Feats Alertness, Combat Reflexes, Dodge, Improved Initiative, Iron Will, Weapon Focus (bite)
Skills Acrobatics +17, Perception +20, Sense Motive +20, Stealth +16, Survival +17
Languages Common, Sylvan

Avalanche (Su) Once every 1d4 rounds as a swift action, the elemental adder can conjure a massive boulder that flies travels in a 120-ft. line before instantly disappearing. The stones deal 6d6 points of damage to all creatures in the line and knocks them prone. A successful DC 20 Reflex save halves the damage and negates being knocked prone. The save DC is Constitution-based.

Poison (Ex) Bite—injury; *save* Fort DC 20; *frequency* 1/round for 6 rounds; *effect* 1d3 Con; *cure* 2 consecutive save. The save DC is Constitution-based

Emerald Naga

An emerald naga is a long snake with glittering viridian scales that appear to be dusted with crushed gems. A large yet exquisite feminine human face tops the thickly muscled snake body. Fangs clearly protrude from the creature's mouth. These creatures can be friendly if approached cautiously. They are intelligent and curious.

Emerald Naga — CR 6

XP 2,400
LN Large aberration
Init +4; **Senses** darkvision 60 ft., low-light vision; **Perception** +13

AC 20, touch 14, flat-footed 15 (+4 Dex, +1 dodge, +6 natural, −1 size)
hp 68 (8d8+32)
Fort +6; **Ref** +8; **Will** +10
SR 17

Speed 40 ft.
Melee bite +10 (2d6+6 plus grab), tail +7 (1d8+4 plus grab)
Special Attacks constrict (tail, 1d8+12)

Abilities Str 18, Dex 19, Con 18, Int 13, Wis 14, Cha 10
Base Atk +6; **CMB** +11; **CMD** 26 (can't be tripped)
Feats Blind-Fight, Dodge, Iron Will, Lightning Reflexes, Skill Focus (Stealth), Weapon Focus (bite)
Skills Bluff +4, Diplomacy +4, Knowledge (arcana) +5, Knowledge (nature) +9, Perception +13, Spellcraft +8, Stealth +14
Languages Common, Draconic

Emerald Naga, Juvenile

A juvenile emerald naga is a seven-foot-long snake with glittering viridian scales that appear to be dusted with crushed gems. A large yet exquisite feminine human face tops the thickly muscled snake body. The face appears to be that of an adolescent human female. Fangs clearly protrude from the creature's mouth. These creatures can be friendly if approached cautiously. They are intelligent and curious.

Juvenile Emerald Naga — CR 3

XP 800
LN Medium aberration
Init +4; **Senses** darkvision 60 ft., low-light vision; **Perception** +11

AC 20, touch 16, flat-footed 15 (+5 Dex, +1 dodge, +4 natural)
hp 39 (6d8+12)
Fort +4; **Ref** +8; **Will** +7
SR 14

Speed 40 ft.
Melee bite +7 (1d8+3), tail +4 (1d6+1)

Abilities Str 14, Dex 21, Con 14, Int 13, Wis 14, Cha 10
Base Atk +4; **CMB** +6; **CMD** 21 (can't be tripped)
Feats Blind-Fight, Dodge, Lightning Reflexes, Skill Focus (Stealth), Weapon Focus (bite)
Skills Bluff +4, Diplomacy +4, Knowledge (arcana) +5, Knowledge (nature) +7, Perception +11, Spellcraft +6, Stealth +12
Languages Common, Draconic

Emerald Naga Queen

The emerald naga queen's viridian brilliance illuminates the area around her. Her emerald scales gleam with exceptional clarity. A lithe and supple snake body rises to the symmetrical face of a woman with high cheekbones and a thin-lipped mouth with the bare hint of fangs. Her head is larger than that of a humanoid and is proportional to her 30-foot-long body. Her tail flicks and even idly manipulates nearby objects as her wide smile and cool gaze surveys any before her.

Emerald Naga Queen — CR 11

XP 12,800
LN Huge aberration
Init +7; **Senses** darkvision 60 ft.; **Perception** +27

AC 26, touch 11, flat-footed 23 (+3 Dex, +15 natural, −2 size)
hp 133 (14d8+70)
Fort +9; **Ref** +9; **Will** +15
SR 21

Speed 40 ft.
Melee bite +15 (2d6+6 plus grab), tail +12 (2d6+3 plus grab)
Space 15 ft.; **Reach** 15 ft.
Special Attacks constrict (tail, 2d6+9), phase strike
Spells Known (CL 9th; concentration +13)
4th (5/day)— *charm monster* (DC 18), *phantasmal killer* (DC 18)
3rd (7/day)— *dispel magic*, *fireball*, *suggestion* (DC 17)
2nd (7/day) — *blur*, *hold person* (DC 16), *invisibility*, *scorching ray*
1st (7/day) — *charm person* (DC 15), *color spray*, *fog cloud*, *mage armor*, *magic missile*
0 (at will)—*daze* (DC 14), *detect magic*, *flare* (DC 14), *mage hand*, *message*, *open/close*, *read magic*, *touch of fatigue*

Abilities Str 23, Dex 17, Con 21, Int 18, Wis 22, Cha 19
Base Atk +10; **CMB** +18 (+22 grapple); **CMD** 31 (can't be tripped)
Feats Alertness, Blind-Fight, Combat Casting, Combat Reflexes, Eschew Materials[B], Improved Initiative, Lightning Reflexes, Weapon Focus (bite)
Skills Acrobatics +20 (+24 when jumping), Bluff +18, Diplomacy +18, Knowledge (arcana) +18, Knowledge (history) +11, Knowledge (Nobility) +11, Perception +27, Sense Motive +24, Stealth +12
Languages Common, Draconic

Phase Strike (Su) Once every 1d4 rounds as a standard action, the emerald naga queen can shed fragments from her scales in a 30-ft. radius spread centered on her. The fragments deal 8d6 points of damage to all creatures in the area and knocks them prone. A successful DC 22 Reflex save halves the damage and negates being knocked prone. The save DC is Constitution-based.
Spells The emerald naga queen casts spells as a 9th-level sorcerer.

Fey Lord

This refined young lord exudes an aura of command and grace, and those around him seem compelled to obey. He looks down upon those around him with a haughty look of derision that makes it clear you are less than he. He wears a set of field plate that is nearly formfitting and seems to hug his body. The glint of golden mail sparkles between the armored plates.

Fey Lord   CR 9

XP 6,400
CN Medium fey
Init +2; **Senses** low-light vision; **Perception** +21

AC 23, touch 12, flat-footed 23 (+10 armor, +1 Dex, +1 dodge, +2 shield)
hp 105 (14d6+56)
Fort +8; **Ref** +13; **Will** +13
DR 10/cold iron; **Immune** mind-affecting effects

Speed 30 ft.
Melee *+1 longsword* +11/+6/+1 (1d8+4/19–20)
Special Attacks disarming charm
Spell-Like Abilities (CL 14th; concentration +20)
At will — *detect thoughts* (DC 20), *sleep* (DC 20), *slow* (DC 20)
3/day — *blindness/deafness* (DC 20), *clairvoyance*, *dimension door*, *haste*, *ice storm*

Abilities Str 16, Dex 15, Con 18, Int 15, Wis 19, Cha 22
Base Atk +7; **CMB** +10; **CMD** 23
Feats Acrobatic Steps, Blind-Fight, Combat Reflexes, Dodge, Lightning Reflexes, Mobility, Nimble Moves
Skills Escape Artist +13, Handle Animal +20, Intimidate +20, Knowledge (arcana) +16, Knowledge (nature) +19, Perception +21, Stealth +13, Survival +18
Languages Common, Sylvan
Equipment *+1 full plate*, *+1 longsword*
SQ bolster troops, for your liege, touché

Bolster Troops (Su) Once per day as a swift action, the fey lord can cure 5d8 points of damage to one ally he can see within 30 feet of him.
Disarming Charm (Sp) The fey lord can bring a humanoid opponent to heel as a standard action. Anyone the fey lord targets must succeed on a Will save or fall instantly under the fey lord's influence, as though by a *charm person* spell (caster level 14th). The ability has a range of 30 feet. At the GM's discretion, the ability might be able to affect different creature types.
For Your Liege Once per day as an immediate action, the fey lord can redirect a spell or effect targeting him to an ally within 30 feet of him. The spell or effect must require a saving throw, and the fey lord must make his decision to redirect the spell or effect prior to attempting the saving throw himself.
Touché Whenever another creature hits the fey lord with a melee attack, he can immediately make an attack of opportunity against that opponent.

Fey Lupe

The dark eyes of these long-limbed wolf-like creatures betray their intelligence. They hunt in packs, using stealth and teamwork to dispatch a foe. They often serve as bodyguards and soldiers for stronger fey creatures. Their thick fur is often painted with dark red symbols and runes, some still dripping in the blood of their victims.

Fey Lupe   CR 1

XP 400
LE Medium fey
Init +2; **Senses** low-light vision, scent; **Perception** +11

AC 15, touch 12, flat-footed 13 (+2 Dex, +3 natural)
hp 13 (3d6+3)
Fort +2; **Ref** +5; **Will** +4

Speed 30 ft.
Melee bite +4 (1d6+2), 2 claws +3 (1d4+1)
Special Attacks pounce

Abilities Str 14, Dex 15, Con 12, Int 6, Wis 13, Cha 9
Base Atk +1; **CMB** +3; **CMD** 15 (19 vs. trip)
Feats Skill Focus (Perception), Weapon Focus (bite)
Skills Acrobatics +9, Perception +11, Stealth +9
Languages Common, Sylvan

Gnaddr

This refined young lord exudes an aura of command and grace, and those around him seem compelled to obey him. He looks down upon those around him with a haughty look of derision that makes it clear you are less than him. He wears a set of field plate that is nearly formfitting and seems to hug his body. The glint of golden mail sparkles between the armored plates.

Gnaddr   CR 8

XP 4,800
CN Medium fey
Init +9; **Senses** low-light vision; **Perception** +17

AC 22, touch 11, flat-footed 21 (+10 armor, +1 Dex, +1 natural)
hp 95 (10d6+60)
Fort +13; **Ref** +19; **Will** +16
DR 10/cold iron; **Immune** mind-affecting effects

Speed 30 ft.
Melee *+1 keen silver dagger* +11/+6/+1 (1d4+4/17–20)
Special Attacks impertinent cur, summon fey
Spell-Like Abilities (CL 10th; concentration +15)
At will — *alter self, entropic shield*
3/day — *dominate person* (DC 20), *mirror image, mislead, ray of exhaustion* (DC 18)
1/day — *flesh to stone* (DC 21)

Abilities Str 16, Dex 21, Con 20, Int 13, Wis 18, Cha 21
Base Atk +5; **CMB** +10; **CMD** 28
Feats Agile Maneuvers, Deceitful, Improved Initiative, Toughness, Weapon Finesse
Skills Bluff +22, Diplomacy +18, Disguise +7, Escape Artist +13, Knowledge (nobility) +7, Knowledge (planes) +9, Perception +17, Perform (wind instruments) +13, Perform (sing) +13, Sense Motive +11, Stealth +13
Languages Common, Sylvan
Equipment *+1 full plate, +1 keen silver dagger, torc na goineog* (see **Appendix B**)

Impertinent cur (Ex) Three times per day Gnaddr can infuse potent poison into his dagger as a swift action.
Gnaddr Poison — injury; *save* Fort DC 20; *frequency* 1/round for 6 rounds; *effect* 1d4 Constitution damage; *cure* 2 consecutive saves. The save DC is Constitution-based.
Summon Fey (Su) Once per day, Gnaddr can call forth 1d6 fey lupes as a standard action. These creatures arrive in 2d6 rounds and serve Gnaddr for up to 1 hour.

Lady Puinseann

Lady Puinseann is a lithe, armor-clad warrior who moves with the grace of a jungle cat and wields her pike with a matching deadliness.

Lady Puinseann   CR 7

XP 3,200
CN Medium fey
Init +5; **Senses** low-light vision; **Perception** +14

AC 22, touch 16, flat-footed 15 (+5 armor, +5 Dex, +1 dodge)
hp 76 (8d6+48)
Fort +14; **Ref** +18; **Will** +16
DR 10/cold iron; **Immune** mind-affecting effects

Speed 30 ft.
Melee *+1 longspear* +10/+5 (1d8+5 plus 1d6 electricity/x3)
Spell-Like Abilities (CL 8th, concentration +14)
At will — *expeditious retreat*
3/day — *blindness/deafness* (DC 18), *mirror image, slow* (DC 18)

Abilities Str 18, Dex 21, Con 20, Int 16, Wis 17, Cha 21
Base Atk +4; **CMB** +8; **CMD** 23
Feats Dodge, Power Attack, Toughness, Weapon Focus (longspear)
Skills Diplomacy +16, Escape Artist +16, Handle Animal +13, Heal +11, Knowledge (planes) +14, Perception +14, Sense Motive +14, Stealth +16, Survival +14
Languages Common, Sylvan
Equipment mithral chain shirt, *+1 shock longspear*

Seanche

This cursed bard's mournful songs are often the only glimpse of him you obtain if you encounter him outside of a tavern or stage. He is a human with pleasing features, sparkling green eyes, and a well-trimmed red beard that matches his light red hair.

Seanche   CR 8

XP 4,800
Human bard 9
CG Medium humanoid (human)
Init +1; **Senses** Perception +9

AC 15, touch 12, flat-footed 13 (+3 armor, +2 Dex)
hp 62 (9d8+18)
Fort +4; **Ref** +8; **Will** +8; +4 vs. bardic performance, language-dependent, and sonic

Speed 30 ft.
Melee *+1 rapier* +9/+4 (1d6+1/18–20)
Special Attacks bardic performance 24 rounds/day (move action; countersong, dirge of doom, distraction, fascinate, inspire competence +3, inspire courage +2, inspire greatness, *suggestion*
Bard Spells Known (CL 9th, concentration +13)
3rd (4/day) — *clairaudience/clairvoyance, displace, haste, see invisibility*
2nd (5/day) — *animal messenger, cure moderate wounds, sound burst* (DC 18), *summon swarm*
1st (6/day) — *alarm, charm person* (DC 17), *disguise self, hideous laughter* (DC 17), *unseen servant*
0-level (at will) — *detect magic, light, lullaby* (DC 16), *message, read magic, summon instrument*

Abilities Str 10, Dex 14, Con 12, Int 14, Wis 14, Cha 18
Base Atk +6; **CMB** +6; **CMD** 18
Feats Arcana Strike, Silent Spell, Skill Focus (Perform [wood instruments]), Still Spell, Toughness, Weapon Finesse
Skills Appraise +10, Bluff +14, Intimidate +10, Knowledge (arcana) +15, Knowledge (dungeoneering, engineering, geography, local, nature, nobility, religion) +10, Knowledge (history) +13, Knowledge (planes) +18, Linguistics +8, Perception +9, Perform (sing) +14, Perform (wood instruments) +21, Profession (cobbler) +6, Sense Motive +9, Spellcraft +14, Stealth +15, Use Magic Device +18
Languages Common, Celestial, Dwarven, Infernal, Sylvan
Equipment masterwork studded leather armor, *+1 rapier, Uilleann Pipes of Reality*

Shadow Seanche

This magical doppelganger of the Seanche behaves just like the original. It is fully aware that it is a duplicate.

Shadow Seanche   CR 10

XP 9,600
Pathfinder Roleplaying Game Bestiary 3 "Fey Creature" template
Pathfinder Roleplaying Game Bestiary 4 "Shadow Creature" template
Outsider (augmented fey) bard 9
CE Medium outsider (augmented fey)
Init +1; **Senses** low-light vision; **Perception** +9

AC 17, touch 14, flat-footed 13 (+3 armor, +4 Dex)
hp 62 (9d8+18)
Fort +4; **Ref** +10; **Will** +8; +4 vs. bardic performance, language-dependent, and sonic
DR 5/cold iron and magic; **Resist** cold 10, electricity 10, fire 10
SR 15

Speed 30 ft., fly 45 ft. (good)
Melee rapier +10/+5 (1d6–1/18–20)
Special Attacks bardic performance 24 rounds/day (move action; countersong, dirge of doom, distraction, fascinate, inspire competence +3, inspire courage +2, inspire greatness, *suggestion*)
Spell-Like Abilities
3/day — *dancing lights*
1/day — *confusion* (DC 15), *deep slumber* (DC 13), *entangle* (DC 11), *faerie fire*, *glitterdust*, *major image*
Bard Spells Known (CL 9th, concentration +13)
3rd (4/day) — *clairaudience/clairvoyance, displace, haste, see invisibility*
2nd (5/day) — *animal messenger, cure moderate wounds, sound burst* (DC 18), *summon swarm*
1st (6/day) — *alarm, charm person* (DC 17), *disguise self, hideous laughter* (DC 17), *unseen servant*
0-level (at will) — *detect magic, light, lullaby* (DC 16), *message, read magic, summon instrument*

Abilities Str 8, Dex 18, Con 12, Int 16, Wis 14, Cha 20
Base Atk +6; **CMB** +6; **CMD** 20
Feats Arcana Strike, Silent Spell, Skill Focus (Perform [wood instruments]), Still Spell, Toughness, Weapon Finesse
Skills Appraise +11, Bluff +15, Intimidate +11, Knowledge (arcana) +16, Knowledge (dungeoneering, engineering, geography, local, nature, nobility, religion) +11, Knowledge (history) +14, Knowledge (planes) +19, Linguistics +9, Perception +9, Perform (sing) +15, Perform (wood instruments) +22, Profession (cobbler) +6, Sense Motive +9, Spellcraft +15, Stealth +17, Use Magic Device +19
Languages Common, Celestial, Dwarven, Infernal, Sylvan
SQ evasion, shadow blend
Equipment masterwork studded leather armor, rapier

Shadow Blend (Su) In any illumination other than bright light, a shadow creature blends into the shadows, giving it concealment (20% mikss chance). A shadow creature can suspend or resume this ability as a free action.

Playing the Seanche

This cursed bard's goal is always to escape any sort of combat. He uses spells to hide and then quickly slips away. He relies upon the *uilleann pipes of destiny* in order to aid his escape, and he avoids direct physical combat. The Seanche is a spellcaster and relies upon his prepared spells to evade and disorient his enemies. He is loath to use actions that permanently harm his opponents and uses his skill with illusions to trap his enemies while he escapes. One of his classic ploys is to first cast an illusory double directly on top of himself using *seeming*. He then uses *invisibility* on his next turn to run away while his double heads the other way. Be clever with his actions and remember that above all, his goal is to escape.

Severed Shadow

This is the malicious shadow of a creature that seeks to destroy its material counterpart so it can remain in its stead. It has Seanche's base statistics with the fey and shadow templates.

Steel Elf (Fandir)

Steel elves, also sometimes called fandirs, are an offshoot of the elven race that dwell on the Plane of Molten Skies and rarely venture forth from their home in the Steel Garden (a jungle composed of living metal plants). Steel elves average five feet tall and typically weigh just over 100 pounds. Their skin is glossy silver and their hair ranges from silver to bronze to brass to gold. Eye color varies, though most tend to be a shade of bronze or brass.

Steel Elf — CR 1/4

XP 100
Steel elf warrior 1
N Medium humanoid (elf)
Init +1; **Senses** low-light vision; **Perception** +9

AC 14, touch 11, flat-footed 13 (+3 armor, +1 Dex)
hp 5 (1d8+1)
Fort +3; **Ref** +3; **Will** +2; +2 vs. enchantment
Immune sleep

Speed 30 ft.
Melee longsword +3 (1d8+1/19–20)
Ranged longbow +2 (1d8/x3)

Abilities Str 12, Dex 12, Con 12, Int 10, Wis 12, Cha 10
Base Atk +1; **CMB** +2; **CMD** 13
Feats Weapon Focus (longsword)
Skills Perception +4, Stealth +2; **Racial Modifiers** +2 Perception
Languages Common, Elven
Equipment studded leather armor, longsword, longbow, 20 arrows

Summer Knight

The summer knight is a fey creature bound to the summer court. Its voice is like honey, its smile a beam of light. Grace and the swiftness and ferocity of a jungle cat are wrapped in the charming and warm exterior of the handsome elfin humanoid. It controls the natural magic of the world around it with ease.

Summer Knight — CR 3

XP 800
LN Medium fey
Init +3; **Senses** low-light vision; **Perception** +12

AC 19, touch 14, flat-footed 15 (+5 armor, +3 Dex, +1 dodge)
hp 38 (7d6+14)
Fort +4; **Ref** +8; **Will** +7
DR 5/cold iron; SR 9

Speed 30 ft.
Melee mwk longsword +6 (1d8+4/19–20), mwk dagger +6 (1d4+2/19–20)
Spell Like Abilities (CL 4th, concentration +8)
3/day — *lesser restoration*

Abilities Str 19, Dex 17, Con 14, Int 12, Wis 14, Cha 19
Base Atk +3; **CMB** +7; **CMD** 21
Feats Dodge, Mobility, Power Attack, Two-Weapon Fighting
Skills Bluff +16, Disguise +16, Escape Artist +13, Knowledge (nature) +11, Perception +12, Stealth +13, Use Magic Device +14
Languages Common, Sylvan
Equipment silver armor (masterwork chainmail), masterwork longsword, masterwork dagger
SQ knight's favor

Knight's Favor (Su) Three times per day, the summer knight can grant a +2 luck bonus to any ally's attack roll or saving throw within 30 feet as an immediate action.

Appendix B: New Magic Items

New magic items found in this adventure are described in this appendix.

Brighid's Raiment and Arms

Brighid's Breastplate
Aura moderate abjuration; **CL** 9th
Slot armor; **Price** 8,500 gp; **Weight** 35 lbs.

This bronze *+1 breastplate* is etched in flame-like patterns of rams facing one another, heads lowered to charge. The breastplate is remarkably light and if you are of good alignment, it emits a soft golden glow. While you wear this armor, you gain fire resistance 10 and a +2 resistance bonus to saving throws against enchantment spells and effects.
Requirements Craft Magic Arms and Armor, *resist energy*; **Cost** 4,250 gp

Brighid's Spear
Aura faint evocation; **CL** 6th
Slot –; **Price** 4,300 gp; **Weight** 6 lbs.
The spearhead is about 20 inches long and has a "flame blade" of shallow waves. It shows signs of use in the many nicks and scratches in the metal. It attaches to a six-and-a-half-foot hardwood pole to create a *+1 spear*. Once per day, you can use a swift action to cause the spearhead to burst into flames, dealing an additional 8d6 fire damage to creature you hit with the spear.
Requirements Craft Magical Arms and Armor, *flaming sphere*; **Cost** 2,150 gp

Brighid's Shield
Aura faint abjuration; **CL** 6th
Slot shield; **Price** 7,630 gp; **Weight** 10 lbs.
Brighid's *+1 heavy shield* gleams when lifted and is difficult to look at for long because of the reflected light. Once per day as a standard action, you may use the shield to cast *daylight*.
Requirements Craft Magical Arms and Armor, *daylight*; **Cost** 3,815 gp

---

Deadly Whisper

Aura faint enchantment and illusion; **CL** 6th
Slot –; **Price** 15,300 gp; **Weight** 2 lbs.
This elegantly crafted *+1 shortsword* slices the air with barely a whisper, and the pommel is adorned with a gleaming black opal that seems to drink the light around it. Three times per day as a standard action, you may speak a command word to cause the rapier to cast *silence* centered on the blade.
Requirements Craft Magical Arms and Armor, *silence*; **Cost** 7,650 gp

Feyslayer Sword

Aura moderate conjuration; **CL** 10th
Slot –; **Price** 12,000 gp; **Weight** 4 lbs.
This heavy, *+1 fey bane longsword* is crafted from meteoric cold iron and always feels cold to the touch. Once per day as an immediate action, you can speak a command word to grant a +5 insight bonus to an ally within 30 feet. If an elf or fey owns the blade, the owner suffers 1 point of Constitution damage at the end of each hour that the sword remains in the owner's possession.
Requirements Craft Magical Arms and Armor, *summon monster I*, *true strike*; **Cost** 6,000 gp

Leprechaun's Gold

Aura faint transmutation; **CL** 6th
Slot –; **Price** 400 gp; **Weight** varies

Leprechaun's gold is a group of saucer-sized gold coins with a great glyph on one face and a snake eating its tail on the opposite face. If a creature other than the leprechaun who owns the coins opens their container, the coins immediately polymorph into a cloud of tiny golden-winged snakes that attempt to hide. A creature may spot the fleeing snakes with a Perception check. The number of coins (snakes) spotted depends on the DC of the check per the table below.

DC	Coins Spotted
15	1
18	2
20	4
22	7
25	13

Once spotted, the person who opened the container may use a move action to grab one of the snakes. Doing so requires a successful DC 15 Acrobatics check. Once captured, a flying snake reverts to a coin that is worth 10 gp. They are usually found in caches of 1d100 + 8 coins. If they are gathered in a group of nine or more coins, they attempt to escape and hide again. They always try to escape to their original owner.

Requirements Craft Wondrous Item, *mislead*; **Cost** 200 gp

Luricawne Shoes

Aura faint enchantment; **CL** 8th
Slot feet; **Weight** 2 lbs.

These exquisitely crafted shoes conform to the feet of any creature from Tiny to Large. When a living creature puts on the shoes, a magical curse immediately forcibly compels that creature to use its standard action to dance, causing it to make a Perform (dance) check each round against DC 20. On a success, the creature's dancing skill destroys the footwear and frees the wearer from the curse. Otherwise, the shoes cannot be removed by any means short of a *remove curse*, *break enchantment* spell or similar magic.

Magic Items *boots of elvenkind, boots of levitation, boots of speed, boots of striding and springing, winged boots*

Torc na Goineog

Aura moderate conjuration and transmutation; **CL** 12th
Slot head; **Price** 36,500 gp; **Weight** 1 lb.
Wondrous item, legendary (requires attunement)

The torc of the serpents is said to signify its wearer as the king of serpents and grants commensurate power. While wearing the torc, the wearer gains a +2 resistance bonus to Reflex saving throws and immunity to poison. The wearer can also *speak with animals* (snakes only) at will as the *speak with animals* spell, and can *dominate animal* (as the *dominate animal* spell, snakes only) and summon a constrictor snake (as the *summon nature's ally III* spell) three times per day as a standard action. Once per week, the wearer can cast *beast shape I* to transform into a constrictor snake or a venomous snake (*Pathfinder Roleplaying Game Bestiary*).

Requirements Craft Wondrous Item, *beast shape I, dominate animal*; **Cost** 18,250 gp

Uillean Pipes of Reality

Aura moderate transmutation; **CL** 14th
Slot –; **Price** 46,250 gp; **Weight** 8 lbs.

The *Uillean pipes of reality*'s owner can use a standard action to cause a single song of the owner's choice to manifest into reality once per day. The magic of the pipes approximates the song with as close a proxy as it can identify. The uillean pipes compel the owner to constantly travel, magically compelling him from staying in the same town, village, or camp twice. The owner must perform before a crowd at least once per day, and the owner must perform a song of the pipes' choosing during that performance. The pipes' owner may use a standard action to cast the following spells.

At will: *expeditious retreat, pass without trace*
3/day: *dimension door*

Furthermore, whenever an opponent attempts to directly attack the piper's owner, even with a targeted spell, the pipes emit an awful sound that forces all living creatures within 60-foot radius spread to succeed on a DC 16 Fortitude saving throw or be paralyzed for 1 minute. The pipes cannot emit this note more than three times per hour. This is a sonic, mind-affecting effect.

Requirements Craft Wondrous Item, *dimension door, song of discord*; **Cost** 23,125 gp

Product Identity: The following items are hereby identified as Frog God Games LLC's Product Identity, as defined in the Open Game License version 1.0a, Section 1(e), and are not Open Game Content: product and product line names, logos and identifying marks including trade dress; artifacts; creatures; characters; stories, storylines, plots, thematic elements, dialogue, incidents, language, artwork, symbols, designs, depictions, likenesses, formats, poses, concepts, themes and graphic, photographic and other visual or audio representations; names and descriptions of characters, spells, enchantments, personalities, teams, personas, likenesses and special abilities; places, locations, environments, creatures, equipment, magical or supernatural abilities or effects, logos, symbols, or graphic designs; and any other trademark or registered trademark clearly identified as Product Identity. Previously released Open Game Content is excluded from the above list.

Notice of Open Game Content: This product contains Open Game Content, as defined in the Open Game License, below. Open Game Content may only be Used under and in terms of the Open Game License.

Designation of Open Game Content: Subject to the Product Identity Designation herein, the following material is designated as Open Game Content. (1) all monster statistics, descriptions of special abilities, and sentences including game mechanics such as die rolls, probabilities, and/or other material required to be open game content as part of the game rules, or previously released as Open Game Content, (2) all portions of spell descriptions that include rules-specific definitions of the effect of the spells, and all material previously released as Open Game Content, (3) all other descriptions of game-rule effects specifying die rolls or other mechanic features of the game, whether in traps, magic items, hazards, or anywhere else in the text, (4) all previously released Open Game Content, material required to be Open Game Content under the terms of the Open Game License, and public domain material anywhere in the text.

Use of Content from Tome of Horrors Complete: This product contains or references content from the Tome of Horrors Complete by Frog God Games. Such content is used by permission and an abbreviated Section 15 entry has been approved. Citation to monsters from the Tome of Horrors Complete or other monster Tomes must be done by citation to that original work.

OPEN GAME LICENSE Version 1.0a

The following text is the property of Wizards of the Coast, Inc. and is Copyright 2000 Wizards of the Coast, Inc. ("Wizards"). All Rights Reserved.

1. Definitions: (a) "Contributors" means the copyright and/or trademark owners who have contributed Open Game Content; (b) "Derivative Material" means copyrighted material including derivative works and translations (including into other computer languages), potation, modification, correction, addition, extension, upgrade, improvement, compilation, abridgement, or other form in which an existing work may be recast, transformed, or adapted; (c) "Distribute" means to reproduce, license, rent, lease, sell, broadcast, publicly display, transmit, or otherwise distribute; (d) "Open Game Content" means the game mechanic and includes the methods, procedures, processes, and routines to the extent such content does not embody the Product Identity and is an enhancement over the prior art and any additional content clearly identified as Open Game Content by the Contributor, and means any work covered by this License, including translations and derivative works under copyright law, but specifically excludes Product Identity; (e) "Product Identity" means product and product line names, logos, and identifying marks including trade dress; artifacts; creatures and characters; stories, storylines, plots, thematic elements, dialogue, incidents, language, artwork, symbols, designs, depictions, likenesses, formats, poses, concepts, themes, and graphic, photographic, and other visual or audio representations; names and descriptions of characters, spells, enchantments, personalities, teams, personas, likenesses, and special abilities; places, locations, environments, creatures, equipment, magic or supernatural abilities or effects, logos, symbols, or graphic designs; and any other trademark or registered trademark clearly identified as Product Identity by the owner of the Product Identity, and which specifically excludes the Open Game Content; (f) "Trademark" means the logos, names, mark, sign, motto, designs that are used by a Contributor to identify itself or its products or the associated products contributed to the Open Game License by the Contributor; (g) "Use", "Used", or "Using" means to use, Distribute, copy, edit, format, modify, translate, and otherwise create Derivative Material of Open Game Content; (h) "You" or "Your" means the licensee in terms of this agreement.

2. The License: This License applies to any Open Game Content that contains a notice indicating that the Open Game Content may only be Used under and in terms of this License. You must affix such a notice to any Open Game Content that you Use. No terms may be added to or subtracted from this License except as described by the License itself. No other terms or conditions may be applied to any Open Game Content distributed using this License.

3. Offer and Acceptance: By Using the Open Game Content You indicate Your acceptance of the terms of this License.

4. Grant and Consideration: In consideration for agreeing to use this License, the Contributors grant You a perpetual, worldwide, royalty-free, non-exclusive license with the exact terms of this License to Use, the Open Game Content.

5. Representation of Authority to Contribute: If You are contributing original material as Open Game Content, You represent that Your Contributions are Your original creation and/or You have sufficient rights to grant the rights conveyed by this License.

6. Notice of License Copyright: You must update the COPYRIGHT NOTICE portion of this License to include the exact text of the COPYRIGHT NOTICE of any Open Game Content You are copying, modifying, or distributing, and You must add the title, the copyright date, and the copyright holder's name to the COPYRIGHT NOTICE of any original Open Game Content you Distribute.

7. Use of Product Identity: You agree not to Use any Product Identity, including as an indication as to compatibility, except as expressly licensed in another, independent Agreement with the owner of each element of that Product Identity. You agree not to indicate compatibility or co-adaptability with any Trademark or Registered Trademark in conjunction with a work containing Open Game Content except as expressly licensed in another, independent Agreement with the owner of such Trademark or Registered Trademark. The use of any Product Identity in Open Game Content does not constitute a challenge to the ownership of that Product Identity. The owner of any Product Identity used in Open Game Content shall retain all rights, title, and interest in and to that Product Identity.

8. Identification: If you distribute Open Game Content, You must clearly indicate which portions of the work that you are distributing are Open Game Content.

9. Updating the License: Wizards or its designated Agents may publish updated versions of this License. You may use any authorized version of this License. You may use any authorized version of this License to copy, modify, and distribute any Open Game Content originally distributed under any version of this License.

10. Copy of this License: You MUST include a copy of this License with every copy of the Open Game Content You Distribute.

11. Use of Contribute Credits: You may not market or advertise the Open Game Content using the name of any Contributor unless You have written permission from the Contributor to do so.

12. Inability to Comply: If it is impossible for You to comply with any of the terms of this License with respect to some or all of the Open Game Content due to statute, judicial order, or governmental regulation then You may not Use any Open Game Material so affected.

13. Termination: This License will terminate automatically if You fail to comply with all terms herein and fail to cure such breach within 30 days of becoming aware of the breach. All sublicenses shall survive the termination of this License.

14. Reformation: If any provisions of this License is held to be unenforceable, such provision shall be reformed only to the extent necessary to make it enforceable.

15. COPYRIGHT NOTICE

Open Game License v 1.0a © 2000, Wizards of the Coast, Inc.

System Reference Document 5.0 © 2016, Wizards of the Coast, Inc.; Authors Mike Mearls, Jeremy Crawford, Chris Perkins, Rodney Thompson, Peter Lee, James Wyatt, Robert J. Schwalb, Bruce R. Cordell, Chris Sims, and Steve Townshend, based on original material by E. Gary Gygax and Dave Arneson.

Pathfinder Roleplaying Game Reference Document. © 2011, Paizo Publishing, LLC; Author: Paizo Publishing, LLC.

Pathfinder Roleplaying Game Core Rulebook. © 2009, Paizo Publishing, LLC; Author: Jason Bulmahn, based on material by Jonathan Tweet, Monte Cook, and Skip Williams.

Original Spell Name Compendium © 2002 Clark Peterson

Seanche's Lament © 2020, Frog God Games; Author Ian McGarty

www.ingramcontent.com/pod-product-compliance
Lightning Source LLC
Chambersburg PA
CBHW041202100726
47911CB00016B/835